TWO SIDES OF THE SAME COIN: WHAT IS HARM?

BOOK I OF THE DR. T'SHAKA MALONE SERIES

First Edition: 2025
Published by

Maat Productions / Publications
Ancient Wisdom. Modern Vision.

Library & Cataloging (Optional Placeholder)
Library of Congress Control Number
Pending

ISBN: 979-8-9932330-2-4

TWO SIDES OF THE SAME COIN

WHAT IS HARM?

BOOK 1 OF THE DR. T'SHAKA MALONE SERIES

Epigraph

"Harm does not always announce itself with violence.

Sometimes it arrives wrapped in necessity,

signed by authority,

and defended by those who believe they are doing good."

— From the Malone Files

TABLE OF CONTENTS

Why Two Sides of the Same Coin Is a Necessary Book

Two Sides of the Same Coin is necessary because the question of **justice** has never been settled—only managed.

Throughout history, justice has often been discussed as though it were neutral, objective, and evenly applied. But the lived experience of marginalized communities—particularly Black communities—tells a different story. Justice, more often than not, has been shaped, delayed, denied, or weaponized by those who hold power.

This book stands in conversation with the legacies of **Ida B. Wells** and **Medgar Evers**, two figures who refused to accept the dominant narrative that justice naturally emerges from institutions. Wells exposed the lie that lynching was about criminality when it was, in fact, about control, fear, and economic suppression. Evers challenged the idea that civil rights could wait for permission, knowing that justice delayed was justice denied.

Both understood something essential:

justice is not abstract—it is contested.

Two Sides of the Same Coin asks the same uncomfortable questions they did:

- Is justice tangible, or is it merely a concept shaped by those with authority?
- Who gets to define harm—and whose suffering is considered acceptable collateral?
- At what point does legality diverge from morality?

Through the character of Dr. T'Shaka Malone, the novel explores justice not as a slogan, but as a **responsibility**. T'Shaka exists inside systems that claim to uphold justice while simultaneously reproducing harm. His brilliance forces those systems to confront their own contradictions. His presence raises a dangerous possibility: what happens when someone understands the rules *and* the history behind them?

Like Wells and Evers, this story refuses comfort. It does not present justice as clean or inevitable. Instead, it frames justice as something that must be **named, defended, and sometimes wrestled back from power itself**.

In an era where violence can be justified by policy and harm can be sanitized by language, *Two Sides of the Same Coin* insists on discernment. It challenges readers to recognize that justice is not simply the absence of wrongdoing, but the courage to confront systems that benefit from silence.

This book is necessary because it reminds us that justice is not a destination—it is a choice.

And choices, as history has shown us, always reveal who we are willing to protect—and who we are willing to sacrifice.

Two Sides of the Same Coin: What Is Harm?

Book One of the Dr. T'Shaka Malone Series

By TJ Debnam

At eighteen years old, **Dr. T'Shaka Malone** is already a paradox.

A prodigy with three PhDs, a Nobel Peace Prize, and a mind capable of reconstructing crime scenes as living holograms, T'Shaka is the youngest FBI field agent in history. Raised with love, anchored by his lifelong partner Christy Jones, and driven by a belief that justice—however imperfect—must be pursued through law, he represents what the system claims it can produce at its best.

But when a federal judge is murdered inside a U.S. courthouse, T'Shaka's first official case pulls him into a darkness the law cannot easily name.

The killer leaves no fingerprints, no weapons, and no clear cause of death—only a disturbing philosophical trail. Victims are powerful, untouchable figures who escaped accountability. The crimes echo a modern Jack the Ripper, but with surgical precision and moral certainty. At the heart of it all is a twisted interpretation of the Hippocratic Oath: *harm must be ended, not avoided.*

As T'Shaka builds the profile, he uncovers a serial killer who does not see himself as a monster, but as a physician correcting a diseased system. Brilliant, disciplined, and dangerously convinced of his righteousness, the killer operates with chilling restraint—until his control is threatened.

Unbeknownst to T'Shaka, the hunt is deeply personal.

Dr. Booker T. Atticus Williams—a genius physician shaped by isolation, manipulation, and systemic betrayal—has been watching the world fail for years. Forged in absence and driven by radical philosophy, Booker believes justice is not something to wait for. It is something to *administer*. The law never protected him. Medicine gave him power. And harm, in his hands, becomes mercy.

As racism, institutional resistance, and political pressure close in—from a hostile Texas sheriff to federal agencies unsure whether to protect or exploit their prodigy—T'Shaka must confront a question no training prepared him for:

When the system causes harm, who decides how it ends?

Two Sides of the Same Coin: What Is Harm is a gripping psychological thriller that explores justice, morality, race, and power through two brilliant men shaped by the same world—and divided by the choices they make. It is the beginning of a high-stakes series where intellect is weaponized, certainty is deadly, and the line between protector and executioner grows dangerously thin.

PROLOGUE
THE FIRST OATH BROKEN

April 10, 1990.

Chicago, Illinois

The operating room smelled of antiseptics and restraints.

Dr. Booker T. Atticus Williams stood at the table for eleven hours straight, hands steady, posture immaculate, eyes unblinking. The procedure—an intricate vascular reconstruction—was the kind of surgery most physicians only read about in journals long after retirement. For Booker, it was simply Tuesday.

The patient lived.

Applause followed. Quiet. Respectful. Professional.

Booker washed his hands for a full three minutes longer than protocol required. Control mattered. Control was everything.

It wasn't until later—after the scrubs were discarded, after the locker door shut with a dull metallic echo—that the control fractured.

A resident spoke in hushed tones in the corridor; voice lowered not out of reverence but convenience.

"Thirteen years old. Judge said there wasn't enough evidence to convict, but you know that money played a role, just how these cases go."

Booker T. stopped walking.

"Who?" he asked.

The name came easily. Too easily. A colleague. A man with credentials, a reputation, a wife who smiled at charity galas. A man who volunteered at clinics in neighborhoods like the little girl came from.

A Black girl.

Thirteen.

The facts assembled themselves in Booker's mind with surgical precision. Timeline. Access. Probability. Outcome.

Acquitted.

That word lodged somewhere behind his sternum, sharp and immovable.

He attended the trial. Sat in the back. Watched the girl avoid eye contact with anyone wearing authority. Watched the defense turn her childhood into a series of convenient inconsistencies. Watched the jury deliberate less time than it took to scrub in.

When the verdict was read, Booker did not react.

Not externally.

Something inside him did not shatter—it *realigned.*

He went home and opened a notebook he had not touched in years. On the first page, he wrote a single line:

If harm is permitted, then prevention must become correction.

He did not plan the first kill.

That was the mistake.

The colleague lived alone in a renovated brownstone. Booker knew his routines. Surgeons were predictable; arrogance bred patterns. Booker arrived with nothing but his hands, a syringe he should not have brought, and an idea he had not fully tested.

The death was ugly.

Too much force. Too much time. A broken lamp. Blood where there should not have been blood.

Booker stood in the aftermath, breathing too fast, heart betraying him. This was not medicine. This was chaos.

And yet—

As the adrenaline receded, something else settled in.

Clarity.

The noise in his mind—the constant calculus of injustice, the unanswered question of *why some harm is allowed to continue*—fell silent.

Control returned.

Not the clean control of the operating room.

A deeper one.

He cleaned the scene poorly. Missed things. Left behind evidence that would later confuse detectives. He did not care. The correction had been made.

Outside, the city went on breathing.

Miles away, in another state, a ten-year-old boy named T'Shaka Malone sat on a front porch, scowling as a girl his age stood over him with hands on her hips.

“Stop thinking so much,” Christy said. “Just do it.”

T’Shaka sighed, grabbed his bike helmet, and obeyed.

He did not know that the world had just tilted.

He did not know that, in Chicago, a man with his same brilliance—but none of his self love—had crossed a line that could not be uncrossed.

And somewhere between justice and silence,

The Hippocratic Ghost was born.

CHAPTER ONE
EIGHT YEARS LATER (1999)

The theatre chairs were uncomfortable for the 6'0 athletic frame of Dr. T'Shaka Malone. Despite this, he remained seated, his posture both relaxed and alert, a familiar stance he adopted when he wished to blend into the background.

The auditorium was alive with the unmistakable energy that accompanies significant endings. Parents whispered quietly among themselves, programs rustled in restless hands, and camera flashes punctuated the air like brief sparks of pride. Above, banners in vibrant school colors hung from the rafters, each boldly proclaiming achievement and promise with hopeful lettering.

Hunters Lane High School was graduating its class of 1999.

And T'Shaka Malone, age eighteen, PhD-holder three times over, bestselling author three times over, youngest consultant the federal government had ever had, clapped just as loudly as everyone else.

Because today wasn't about him.

It was about **Christy Jones**.

Christy walked confidently across the stage, her presence radiating both assurance and authenticity. Moments earlier, she had delivered an inspiring speech, encouraging her classmates to "be the change they wish to see." Her words resonated throughout the Grand Ole Opry Theatre, echoing her belief in action and self-determination.

With her shoulders squared and chin held high, Christy embodied the very ideals she spoke about. Honor cords lay neatly against her graduation gown, signifying her achievements. As the valedictorian and top of her class, she stood as a clear example of dedication and excellence.

When her name was called, the applause that erupted was thunderous and filled with genuine appreciation, not mere courtesy. The audience's response was well earned, reflecting the impact she had made on both her peers and the broader school community. Christy smiled in that familiar way, proud of her accomplishments and unapologetic about celebrating them.

T'Shaka stood.

He didn't mean to. His body moved before his mind could stop it. He clapped until his palms stung and whistled once, sharp and loud, earning a few side glances from parents who had long since learned that the quiet boy with the old soul was not, in fact, an ordinary teenager.

Christy found him in the crowd.

She rolled her eyes, smiling.

Sit down, her look said.

He grinned back.

Eight years ago, she had strongly encouraged him on a porch, hands on her hips, by telling him to stop thinking so much. The dynamic hadn't changed much since, except now the boy she ordered around carried credentials that made professors nervous and federal agencies cautious.

But with Christy, he was still just T'Shaka.

After the ceremony, the gym spilled into noise and motion. Families crowded the floor. Flowers exchanged hands. Tears came easily. Christy's mother hugged her so tightly that her cap slipped sideways. T'Shaka watched, hands in his pockets, content to orbit.

“You could’ve been up there,” someone said nearby, a voice half-admiring, half-accusatory.

T’Shaka smiled politely. “Oh, I had graduated high school when I was twelve.”

That usually ended the conversation.

Christy found him a moment later, diploma in hand, face glowing. “Spellman,” she said, breathless. “*Computer Science.* Atlanta better be ready.”

“They won’t be,” T’Shaka replied. “But they’ll adjust.”

She nudged him with her shoulder. “You always say that.”

“And I’m always right.”

She laughed, looping her arm through his. For all the books written by T’Shaka—*Forensics and the Case for Black Innocence*, *Why There Should Never Be Another George Stinney*, *Inside the Mind of U.S.-Bred Terrorism*—this was the space where he felt more at peace, with family and with Christy Jones.

Miles away, in a quiet Chicago apartment, Dr. Booker T. Williams stood at a kitchen counter while his mother’s voice filled the room.

She spoke the way she always did—measured, cutting, certain.

“Did you see what *he* did now?” she said, lips curled. “Another article. Another headline. Your father’s precious miracle child.”

Booker said nothing.

His mother continued

"That woman raised him to believe the world belongs to him," his mother continued. "The spoiled prince. Given everything. While you—"

Booker's jaw tightened almost imperceptibly. He replied to his mother, "I am one of the youngest surgeons in the U.S., I graduated from Emory, Meharry, and Yale at the top of my class. Mother, I save lives on a daily basis. Besides, it's not my brother and sisters' fault that they do not know I even exist."

Booker T. did not mean to snap at his mother but sometimes she is unfair to his siblings, and her controlling tone really pissed him off at times.

However, he had seen the articles. The awards. Youngest to receive the Nobel Peace prize for *Justice*.

All headlines of his little brother were the same. The prodigy. The youngest. The genius. The boy who proved the system could work if you were exceptional enough to survive it.

His mother continued as if Booker T. did not confront her openly, as she always did, weaving old grievances into fresh resentment, rewriting history until absence looked like abandonment and protection looked like theft.

Booker listened the way surgeons listened—to symptoms, not stories.

He knew better than to believe all of it.

But he also knew this much was true:

Some people were shielded.

Others were forged.

He turned off the light in the kitchen, the glow from the window catching the edge of a folded newspaper on the counter. On it, a photograph of a young man standing beside a graduating girl, both smiling, both untouched by what lurked beneath the surface of the country they lived in.

Booker folded the paper carefully.

In Nashville, Christy Jones leaned up and kissed T'Shaka on his forehead. "You coming to Atlanta with me this weekend?"

"Wouldn't miss it," he said.

Neither of them noticed the way the world seemed, just for a moment, to hold its breath.

Two brothers.

Both celebrated in their own worlds.

But One celebrated with the love of both parents and family.

One watching. All alone, though he had supporters, aunts, uncles, grandfather, community, but the other half that made him true was missing.

And the distance between them—measured not in miles, but in choices—continued to grow.

CHAPTER TWO
QUANTICO

One Month after Graduation

The crack of gunfire echoed across the range, sharp and rhythmic, each report swallowed by the open Virginia air.

The target downrange shuddered once.

Then again.

Then again.

Dead center.

The instructors stopped talking.

Three FBI agents stood shoulder to shoulder with two men from the US Marshals, their conversation trailing off as one of them slowly lowered his binoculars. They watched with growing interest as the events on the range unfolded, the silence between them testament to the gravity of what they were witnessing.

"Are seeing this?" the taller US Marshal asked quietly.

"Every shot," an FBI range master replied. "Forehead. Same spot. He's not correcting recoil—he's anticipating it."

Downrange, the paper target bore a tight cluster of holes so precise they might have been printed there. One more clean hit would shatter a training record that had stood for over a decade.

Dr. T'Shaka Malone exhaled slowly, adjusted his stance by a fraction of an inch, and fired again.

The target jerked.

A murmur rippled through the observers.

Three shots away.

"This is crazy, he is just a kid," one of the Marshals said, incredulous. "He's only eighteen."

The FBI Director regarded the young marksman with calm precision, her tone carrying both admiration and concern. "He should be starting his freshmen year of college or on a date with his girlfriend," she said evenly. "He should enjoy being a young man. Yet it was clear that Dr. T'Shaka Malone was not defined by conventional expectations."

Director Mia Strong's words, though delivered with the authority of her position, radiated the unmistakable warmth of someone who felt a deep, personal pride. "Dr. T'Shaka is beyond exceptional," she added, her expression a blend of protective affection and respect for the young consultant's remarkable achievements.

She stepped forward, hands clasped behind her back, eyes never leaving the young man at the firing line. Pride wasn't something she displayed easily, but today she allowed herself a measure of it.

"That," she said, "is our youngest consultant. Dr. T'Shaka Malone."

The Marshal officers turned.

Director Strong continued, her voice crisp and unwavering as she addressed the assembled officials. "Three earned PhDs," she declared, ensuring that the weight of Dr. Malone's accomplishments was unmistakable. "A PhD in Criminal Psychology, a JD in Law, and a PhD in Forensic Science. All completed before his eighteenth birthday."

She paused for effect, letting the significance sink in. "Each dissertation was published. Each one became a bestseller." Her words highlighted not only the rarity of such academic feats, but also the extraordinary impact Dr. Malone had made across multiple fields at an age when most are just beginning their undergraduate studies.

She glanced down at the file in her hand, though it was clear she knew the details by heart.

- *Forensics and the Case for Black Innocence*
- *Why There Should Never Be Another George Stinney*
- *Inside the Mind of U.S.-Bred Terrorism*

The younger Marshal officer let out a low whistle. "Those books caused congressional hearings."

"They caused reforms," the Director corrected. "And they caused people to finally listen."

Another shot rang out.

Bullseye.

Two shots left.

"What you're about to see," she said, "is why he's here—and why you came all the way from Delaware."

The Marshals leaned in as she continued.

"Malone has a rare cognitive trait. When he walks into a crime scene, he doesn't just observe it. He reconstructs it. Spatial memory, forensic inference, behavioral modeling—it all activates at once. He describes it as watching a hologram assemble itself in real time."

She allowed herself a thin smile as she spoke. “Our top brass calls it impossible. He calls it obvious. Perhaps his greatest attribute lies in his ability to notice every detail—no matter how small or seemingly insignificant.”

Her words carried weight in the silent room, drawing nods from those familiar with Malone’s unique skillset. The Director’s tone was one of admiration, emphasizing how Malone’s attention to detail set him apart. While others dismissed subtle cues or overlooked minor elements, Malone’s focus and ability to discern the smallest nuances often revealed truths that others missed. This unwavering attention became the foundation of his reputation and success.

Another shot.

One left.

“And then there’s this,” she said, nodding toward the range. “Weapons proficiency across platforms. Firearms. Bladed weapons. Tactical systems. He learns patterns faster than we can teach them.”

The older US Marshal shook his head. “That’s not training. That’s intuition.”

“That’s discipline,” the Director said. “And focus.”

The final shot rang out.

Silence followed.

Then the range erupted.

Instructors stared at the target. Agents exchanged looks of disbelief. The range master removed his cap and ran a hand through his hair.

“New record,” he said quietly. “By a wide margin.”

T’Shaka cleared his weapon, movements economical, respectful of protocol. He didn’t smile. He rarely did when the stakes involved numbers instead of people.

He turned and caught sight of the small audience behind the safety glass.

The FBI Director stepped forward as he approached.

“Well done,” she said.

“Thank you, ma’am,” T’Shaka replied.

She turned to the Marshals. “Perhaps most impressive is this—at fifteen, Dr. Malone assisted in solving a murder in Germany while enrolled at Vanderbilt University’s JDP of Law program.”

The younger Marshal officer blinked. “Assisted?”

“He never left Nashville,” she continued. “Reviewed files. Built a psychological profile. Identified inconsistencies in witness statements. Predicted the suspect’s victim selection process.”

“And?” the older officer asked.

“And the suspect confessed after questioning,” she said. “Convicted. Life sentence.”

T’Shaka adjusted his ear protection, gaze steady. “The evidence was sufficient. They just needed to see it arranged correctly.”

The Marshals stared at him now—not as a curiosity, but as an asset.

“Dr. Malone,” the taller one said, extending a hand, “we have a situation. A suspected crime scene that doesn’t make sense to anyone.”

T’Shaka shook his hand once, firmly.

“Then it’s not a crime scene yet,” he said. “It’s just a room full of unanswered questions.”

The Marshal officer smiled slowly.

“We were hoping you’d say that.”

Behind them, unnoticed by anyone, the record board on the wall was quietly updated.

And somewhere far from Quantico, a man with a surgeon’s hands folded a newspaper and felt, without knowing why, the faint pressure of inevitability tightening its grip.

CHAPTER THREE
CHECKLIST

T'Shaka always packed the same way.

Methodical. Ordered. Nothing left to chance.

The bed in his Quantico quarters was a study in meticulous order, with suits folded with near-military precision, a toiletry kit aligned at a perfect right angle, and notebooks stacked carefully by size and purpose, each labeled for its specific use. The space felt less like a teenager's room and more like a command center prepared for a critical mission, every object in place and every detail accounted for. Even the faint scent of fresh linen seemed deliberately maintained, as if T'Shaka's attention to order extended to the very air he breathed.

Christy leaned against the doorframe, arms crossed, a knowing smile tugging at the corners of her mouth. She had just returned to Virginia after completing her summer school courses, eager for a few quiet moments with T'Shaka before the semester began and before he fully immersed himself in the demands of his new case. Watching him now, she couldn't help but feel a mix of admiration and amusement, how the same boy who once stubbornly resisted her instructions on a porch eight years ago now operated with the precision of someone far beyond his years. There was an ease to him in this controlled chaos, a confidence that radiated from his every movement, and Christy found herself both impressed and quietly proud.

"You remember your *Tupac* CD?" she asked.

T'Shaka paused, one sock halfway folded.

"*Me Against the World*," she added pointedly. "Because you think better when Tupac is making magic with metaphors.

He smirked and reached into his carry-on, pulling out the black leather case. "Already packed."

"Good," she said. "And don't forget your lucky pajamas."

He groaned. "They are not—"

"They are," she interrupted. "Every major breakthrough you've ever had, happened while you were wearing those ridiculous Georgetown pajamas."

"They're comfortable," he muttered, placing them carefully on top of his clothes.

"And your Malcolm X T-shirt," Christy continued, moving past him to the dresser. She opened the drawer and held it up. "This one."

"That's not mission attire," he said.

"That's *you* attire," she replied, folding it and handing it to him.

As he reached into the drawer to clear space, something else caught his eye.

A photograph.

Thirteen-year-old versions of them stood frozen in time. He wore a suit carefully made by his grandfather, Clarence, following his uncle's advice that a player always had to stay ready, whatever that meant. Christy couldn't help but wonder if any other girl would have dared to challenge him. She wore a beautiful, fitted dress that she had insisted on, even though everyone else called the dance "corny." On the floor, they moved together as if the world around them had disappeared, the only couple who seemed truly connected, as if they had shared another life somewhere far away.

Because no one else was brave enough to dance in front of teachers.

T'Shaka laughed softly.

"I forgot about that," he said.

Christy smiled, remembering too. "You refused to dance with those girls."

"They called me a nerd, after I politely said no" he said defensively.

"They disrespected my man," she corrected. "So, I corrected *them.*"

"You poured punch on three people."

"They needed hydration."

He shook his head, still smiling. "You almost got suspended."

"Worth it," she said without hesitation.

She crossed to the closet and returned with a shoebox, setting it at the foot of the bed. Inside sat a pristine pair of *Air Jordan 4 Retro White and Gray Cements*, untouched, next to a neatly folded red Lacoste polo.

"You forgot these," she said.

"I didn't forget," he replied. "I was saving them."

"For what?" she asked.

He looked at her. "For when I come back."

The room fell quiet for a moment, the weight of what he didn't say settling between them.

Christy stepped closer. "Just promise me you'll call when you land."

"I always do."

"And don't disappear into your head too much."

"I can't promise that," he said gently. "But I can promise I'll come back."

She reached up, kissed him once—soft, familiar, grounding. The young couple shared a passionate kiss.

Coming up for air.

"I love you, T'Shaka Malone," she said.

He rested his forehead against hers. "I love you too. I'll call when I get to the hotel."

Outside, an engine hummed faintly—the vehicle waiting to take him to the hangar.

Another checklist complete.

Another departure.

Neither of them noticed the way the photograph, half-hidden in the drawer, caught the light—two kids at a dance, unaware of the long shadow their future was already casting.

CHAPTER FOUR
THE OATH TWISTED

The room was quiet in the way only federal offices could be. soundproofed, climate-controlled, stripped of anything that could distract from the work of thinking. Every surface, every corner seemed to exist solely for focus and clarity.

T'Shaka stood alone at the whiteboard, still and measured, every thought locked on the task before him. Case files were spread across the long table behind him, their contents already absorbed, cataloged, and reordered inside his mind. The photographs faced down. He didn't need them anymore. He had seen enough.

"This isn't chaos," he said softly, more to himself than anyone else. "It's revision." His voice carried calm and precision, the quiet confidence of someone who could see the order hidden within what others might call disorder.

He uncapped the marker.

SUBJECT: UNKNOWN

TYPE: SERIAL??? (Perhaps NON-COMPULSIVE)

The FBI analysts watched through the glass, careful not to interrupt. They had learned that when T'Shaka entered this state, the world arranged itself differently around him.

"Is this the first time and what are possible connections? T'Shaka took a deep breath and realized that he had seen this case somewhere before, perhaps once or twice.

He drew a vertical line down the board.

Case 1: Chicago, Illinois, 1990

In 1990, Chicago, Illinois, was the setting for a troubling case involving a doctor accused of molesting a 13-year-old African American child. Despite the severity of the accusation, the doctor was acquitted. However, soon after his innocent verdict, he died peacefully. Notably, a white card was found near his body, an unusual detail that may hold significance.

Case 2: Shelbyville, Tennessee, 1993

Three years later, in 1993, Shelbyville, Tennessee, saw a similar incident. A sheriff, a Caucasian male with considerable local power and influence, was cleared of responsibility in the shooting death of an unarmed 27-year-old Black man. Following his acquittal, the sheriff also died in a peaceful manner, with a white card discovered close to him.

Patterns and Connections

The two cases share striking similarities: both involved Caucasian men in positions of authority who were acquitted of crimes against African American victims, only to die shortly after in circumstances described as peaceful. In both instances, the presence of a white card near the deceased suggests a deliberate, symbolic gesture. This pattern appears to point toward an act of corrective justice, rather than random violence.

He began again.

MOTIVE: MORAL RECTIFICATION

The marker moved quickly now.

The suspect or suspects do not kill for pleasure, nor do they seek attention or recognition for what they do. Their motivation comes from a strong belief: allowing harm to continue without acting is, in their eyes, the same as accepting it. To ignore wrongdoing is to approve it.

At every scene, a white card is left behind, marked with the broken Rod of Asclepius, a symbol long linked to healing, renewal, and the medical principle of "Do No Harm." The damage to the symbol is deliberate. For T'Shaka, the broken Rod shows the opposite of its usual meaning. Instead of protecting life at all costs, the suspect seems to believe that sometimes harm is necessary to prevent greater wrongs. In this way, every action becomes a form of moral correction, a way to stop harm before it can spread further.

T'Shaka paused, his eyes unfocused, not empty, but turned inward. The room around him seemed to fade as the crime scenes formed in his mind: sterile hallways, carefully controlled spaces, and victims who never had a chance to see it coming.

"He has medical training," T'Shaka said. "Advanced. Not just anatomy—pathophysiology. He understands how the body fails quietly."

He sketched a human outline and circled the chest, the brainstem, the pancreas.

"No defensive wounds. No signs of struggle. Death presents as natural or delayed. That tells me he values control—not domination."

One of the analysts leaned forward.

"Meaning?"

"Meaning he doesn't need the victim to know they're dying," T'Shaka replied. "That moment isn't important to him."

He underlined the next words twice.

PHILOSOPHY-DRIVEN

"This killer has rewritten the Hippocratic Oath," he said. "Not 'do no harm'—but 'end harm permanently.'"

The marker clicked against the board as he stepped back.

"He sees himself as a physician of society. The justice system is the disease. His victims are symptoms."

Someone behind the glass exhaled.

T'Shaka continued, voice calm, steady, almost gentle.

"He selects targets who represent systemic failure—people who have escaped accountability. He studies them. Not obsessively. Clinically."

He added another line.

POST-OFFENSE BEHAVIOR: STABLE

"No escalation. No spiraling. Which tells me this isn't compulsion. This is policy."

He capped the marker and folded his arms.

"This is a modern serial killer," he said. "But not one driven by pathology. Driven by certainty."

Silence filled the room.

Finally, an agent spoke through the intercom. "Can he be stopped?"

T'Shaka didn't answer right away.

"Yes," he said at last. "But not by treating him like a monster."

He turned back to the board and wrote the final line.

WEAKNESS: LOSS OF CONTROL

"When his narrative is threatened—when someone proves him wrong, anticipates him, or exposes the flaws in his logic—he will act faster. Sloppier."

He stepped away from the board, the profile complete.

Somewhere far away, in a different city, a man with a surgeon's hands reviewed his own rules and felt—just briefly—the discomfort of being seen without knowing why.

And in the quiet between certainty and correction,

The hunt began.

CHAPTER FIVE
THE FIRST LEAD

June 8, 1999, Waco, Texas, smelled like dust and old authority.

The U.S. courthouse stood at the center of it all, stone-faced and perfectly symmetrical, built to show strength and permanence. Inside, yellow tape stretched across marble floors that had not been touched by violence in decades, marking off areas now filled with quiet tension. Federal agents moved carefully, voices low, their shoes echoing far too loudly in the vast, empty space. Shadows clung to the corners of the hall, and every step seemed to carry the weight of questions no one dared to ask. For T'Shaka, the courthouse was more than a building; it was a place where every detail mattered, and one small mistake could reveal secrets that had long been hidden.

Judge Harold Whitcombe had been found in his chambers just after dawn.

Dead. Apparently, the killer/s had killed the judge during office hours, a risk but calculated.

T'Shaka Malone stood just inside the doorway, hands in his pockets, eyes already working. Two weeks away from Quantico. Two weeks without seeing her before she had gone back to Spellman for the fall semester, without the familiar smell of her perfume lingering in the air, two weeks without the two of them lounging on the couch, doing their own thing but still aware of each other, sharing gentle touches or light ankle rubs after long, tiring days.

Spelman had claimed her now, freshman orientation, new beginnings, a world of experiences that he could only watch from afar. He had told her he was proud. She had told him she loved him and that he was her favorite genius of all time. Even across the distance, the warmth of those words lingered with him, steady and quiet, a reminder of what mattered most.

He didn't need the pressure of being *missed* while trying not to make history the wrong way.

"Dr. Malone," an agent said quietly. "Or—Agent Malone."

T'Shaka nodded once. The title still felt strange.

At eighteen, he was no longer just a consultant brought in to think. This time, the thinking—and the decisions—were his.

"Brief me," he said.

The agent swallowed. "The victim was alone. No forced entry. Security cameras in the hallway were disabled between 2:11 pm and 4:00 p.m. The judge was pronounced dead at the scene. Cause of death pending."

T'Shaka stepped forward.

The room assembled itself in his mind before his feet crossed the threshold.

Judge's desk. Chair slightly off-angle. Coffee cup untouched. Window closed. No signs of struggle. The body lay slumped, expression neutral—almost peaceful.

Too peaceful.

"He didn't die here," T'Shaka said.

The room froze.

The agent blinked. "Sir?"

"He lost consciousness somewhere else," T'Shaka replied calmly. "He was positioned here after. Death occurred sometime later."

"How can you—"

"There's no muscle tension," T'Shaka said. "No defensive response. And the lividity pattern doesn't match where he's sitting. Also, there is no evidence of poison. If there were no poison nor signs of violence, then what was the cause? How did he die? Where did he die?

He crouched, studying the judge's hands.

"No weapon," someone offered.

"No need for one," T'Shaka said.

A voice cut in from behind him, sharp and unimpressed.

"Y'all done yet?"

The Waco County Sheriff filled the doorway, thick build, starched uniform, eyes already dismissing the room and everyone in it. He looked at T'Shaka and smirked.

"Thought the FBI would send someone… older."

T'Shaka stood slowly and turned.

"Dr. Malone," he said evenly. "Lead on this investigation."

The sheriff snorted. "That so?"

"Yes."

The sheriff's gaze lingered too long, too deliberately. "Judge Whitcombe was a good man. Didn't need outsiders stirring things up."

"Judges don't get murdered by accident," T'Shaka replied. "And this wasn't a robbery."

The sheriff crossed his arms. "Are you accusing someone local?"

"I'm accusing someone precise," T'Shaka said. "Which makes this federal."

The tension sharpened.

The sheriff's lips curled in a sneer as he looked T'Shaka up and down. "You think that FBI badge gives you power, boy," he said, his voice tinged with contempt. "And I've seen you before on the TV."

T'Shaka met his eyes without flinching. "Well, Sheriff," he said calmly, "you should understand this. This case happened in a federal building, and I am the lead investigator. Anything you do that I believe is slowing me down or getting in my way will be treated as obstruction of a federal investigation."

He paused, letting the words settle. "And trust me," he added evenly, "I will make sure you are no longer handling security at Chuck E. Cheese. Do I make myself clear?"

The sheriff scoffed and answered, "Yes."

T'Shaka then added, "Yes, what Sheriff?"

"Yes, b..I mean Yes Dr. Malone."

T'Shaka offered a measured smile, one that revealed both the youth in his demeanor and the sharp intelligence behind his eyes. Every word he spoke carried a careful balance of politeness and authority, leaving no room for misunderstanding, no hint of doubt about who held control in the room.

"Thank you, Sheriff, for all your support," he said, calm yet firm. "You may proceed with clearing out the building. I'll let you know when your assistance is needed again."

The Sheriff scoffed, muttered something under his breath, and walked away, his frustration barely contained. T'Shaka watched him go for a moment, noting the tight set of his shoulders and the sharpness in his step, before turning his attention back to the task at hand.

Behind him, Agent Angel Gonzales, a grizzled FBI veteran and T'Shaka's newly assigned partner, shook his head. "You didn't have to poke him," he muttered.

"I didn't," T'Shaka replied evenly, a hint of quiet amusement in his voice. "He did."

Then he turned back to the body, eyes narrowing, mind working a mile a minute. Every detail mattered, the angle of the wound, the position of the hands, the faintest hint of evidence others might overlook. For T'Shaka, this wasn't just a crime scene. It was a puzzle, a story waiting to be read, and he was determined to understand every word.

"No trauma," he said. "No visible injection marks. Which tells me the cause of death will be subtle. Something designed to look natural. Stroke. Heart failure. Something that passes scrutiny unless you're looking for it."

He straightened.

"This killer had access," T'Shaka continued. "Confidence. And time."

Someone asked the question no one wanted to voice.

"You think this is connected to the other cases?"

T'Shaka didn't answer immediately.

He looked around the room one more time, letting the invisible pieces settle into place.

"Yes," he said finally. "But this one's different."

"How?"

"He wanted to be sure the system noticed," T'Shaka replied. "This wasn't a correction in the shadows. This was a statement."

Outside, sirens wailed briefly, then faded.

Miles away, in another city, a man with a surgeon's hands reviewed a headline and allowed himself a single, controlled breath.

The game had changed.

And Dr. T'Shaka Malone—lead agent now, no longer protected by distance—had just stepped fully onto the board.

CHAPTER SIX
THE WORLD REMEMBERS

The room was painfully bright.

Rows of cameras lined the walls, their red lights blinking without rest. Microphones crowded the podium, each stamped with a news network's logo, each waiting to capture a sentence that could become history. The air felt tight, charged with expectation.

Dr. T'Shaka Malone stood just offstage, his hands clasped behind his back, his breathing steady and controlled.

This was not Quantico. This was not a crime scene.

This was a performance.

"Agent Malone," an FBI press aide whispered softly, "they're ready."

T'Shaka gave a single nod.

Moments later, the doors opened.

The quiet murmur of voices rose into a wave of sound as he stepped forward. He stood tall and composed in a dark suit tailored with precision. At just eighteen years old, he was already an FBI field agent, the youngest in the agency's history.

But the world did not see eighteen.

The world saw a memory.

They remembered the headlines that had shaken international news four years earlier:

NOBEL PEACE PRIZE AWARDED TO AMERICAN TEEN PRODIGY U.S. STUDENT SOLVES GERMAN SERIAL MURDER CASE WITHOUT LEAVING NASHVILLE

Standing beside him was FBI Director Mia Strong, her presence offering both approval and protection.

“Ladies and gentlemen,” she said, “you already know Dr. T’Shaka Malone.”

A light wave of laughter moved through the crowd.

“You know him as the youngest Nobel Peace Prize recipient in modern history. At the age of fifteen, while studying at Vanderbilt University, Dr. Malone assisted international authorities in dismantling one of Europe’s most elusive serial murder investigations.”

The large screen behind them came to life.

Grainy black and white crime scene photographs appeared. Redacted reports followed. Then a map of Germany filled the screen, marked with red points scattered across cities and riverbanks.

“Known as the Rhine Silence Case,” Director Strong continued, “this investigation focused on a serial killer the German media named Der Stillmacher, meaning The Silencer.”

The name carried weight.

“His real name was Johannes Kappel.”

T’Shaka remembered the case immediately.

Victims found lifeless in their homes. Lungs collapsed with no visible injury. Deaths labeled as cardiac failure until a disturbing pattern emerged.

Kappel had worked as an anesthesiology technician. He had access, medical knowledge, and precision.

It was T'Shaka's reconstruction of the case, built entirely from files, photographs, and timelines, that exposed the truth.

"He never traveled to Germany," Director Strong said. "Yet Dr. Malone recreated the crime scenes, predicted the offender's behavior, and identified the exact method of murder. Controlled oxygen deprivation using pharmaceutical compounds undetectable in standard toxicology screenings."

She paused, allowing the weight of her words to settle.

"His work led directly to a confession and conviction."

The room erupted in applause.

Camera flashes filled the space like bursts of lightning.

T'Shaka stepped closer to the podium, placing his hands lightly on the microphone.

"I did not solve this case alone," he said evenly. "I listened to what the evidence was already telling us."

Reporters leaned forward.

"Dr. Malone," one voice called out, "how does it feel to be the youngest FBI field agent in U.S. history?"

T'Shaka considered the question carefully.

"It feels like responsibility," he said. "Not privilege."

In Atlanta, inside a Spelman dorm room cluttered with posters, laptops, and half empty coffee cups, Christy sat cross legged on her bed, surrounded by friends.

"That's my T'Shaka Malone," she said with a grin.

She turned her full attention back to the television, her eyes focused, her heart steady.

"That's Dr. T'Shaka Malone," she added with pride. "And don't let the suit fool you. He's tough, and he does real work."

In Nashville, Christy's family gathered in their living room.

Her father nodded slowly as he watched the screen. Her mother quietly wiped tears from her eyes.

"That boy has always been special," her father said.

"He has good people around him," her mother replied. "That's why."

Across town, T'Shaka's family filled their own living room.

Bobby Lee leaned back in his recliner, arms folded, a proud smile spreading across his face.

"That's my son," he said softly.

Beside T'Shaka's mother sat Clarence Malone, his maternal grandfather, a Kangol cap resting across his knees.

"The world is finally seeing what we already knew," Clarence said.

In Chicago, a single television glowed inside a dim apartment.

Dr. Booker T. Atticus Williams sat upright on the edge of a chair, his hands folded neatly, his posture disciplined.

On the screen, T'Shaka spoke with calm authority about justice, restraint, and the danger of absolute certainty.

Booker's mother stood behind him, her arms crossed.

"They praise him," she said sharply. "The favored one. Handed everything."

Booker said nothing.

He studied the young man's eyes. The rhythm of his voice. The discipline behind every word.

There was an intelligence there that felt uncomfortably familiar. He could not yet explain why it unsettled him, or why it stirred a quiet sense of pride.

On the television, a reporter asked the final question.

"Agent Malone," she said, "with your promotion and this new case, what do you believe is the greatest threat to justice today?"

T'Shaka paused.

Then he answered.

"Certainty," he said. "When people decide harm is justified before the law has a chance to speak. I understand why that belief exists, especially when justice seems to abandon the oppressed, the poor, and the disenfranchised."

The words echoed.

In Chicago, Booker's jaw tightened slightly.

Applause filled the room.

Two brothers. One celebrated as the face of justice. One unseen, believing justice had already failed him.

And somewhere between them, fate continued to turn, unaware of which side would rise next.

CHAPTER SEVEN
NAMING THE SHADOW

The room had not settled.

Applause from T'Shaka's final answer still lingered in the air, uneven and restrained, as if the audience sensed the press conference was no longer ceremonial. Something had shifted. What began as formality had turned instructional. The FBI Director adjusted her stance beside him, recognizing the moment when T'Shaka stopped responding to questions and began teaching.

A reporter raised her hand, her voice calm but edged with urgency.

"Agent Malone, is there a pattern to the judge's murder?"

The question hung in the charged silence. The audience leaned forward, aware this was no longer about a single crime. It pressed for clarity, searching for deeper connections, asking whether the murder was isolated or part of a deliberate design.

T'Shaka leaned toward the microphone.

"Yes," he said. "And it did not begin in Waco."

The room fell still.

"What you are seeing," he continued, gesturing toward the screen behind him, "is not a lone homicide. It is the most recent expression of a behavioral pattern that has been evolving for years."

The screen changed.

A timeline appeared, spanning eight years.

Dates. Cities. Names, some visible, others redacted.

"This offender has been active for eight years," T'Shaka said. "Quietly. Selectively. Almost invisibly."

A murmur spread through the press.

"He does not target random civilians," T'Shaka continued. "He targets individuals who represent institutional harm. Judges. Prosecutors. Administrators. Authority figures who, through action or inaction, allowed measurable harm to continue."

A reporter interrupted. "So you are saying he is a vigilante?"

"No," T'Shaka replied evenly. "I am saying he believes he is a physician."

The words settled heavily across the room.

"He does not see himself as violent," T'Shaka said. "He sees himself as corrective."

The screen shifted again.

Chicago.
Shelbyville.
Delaware.
Waco.

Each city appeared beside a single word.

NATURAL.

"These deaths were ruled natural causes," T'Shaka said. "Heart failure. Stroke. Respiratory collapse. No visible trauma. No signs of struggle. No weapon."

He paused.

"And every one of those conclusions was wrong."

The Director did not interrupt. The floor belonged to him now.

"The victims shared a consistent profile," T'Shaka continued. "Each held professional authority. Each faced credible allegations of severe misconduct that never resulted in conviction. Each trusted the system would protect them."

Pens moved rapidly across notebooks.

"This offender possesses advanced medical knowledge," T'Shaka said. "He induces death in ways that imitate spontaneous biological failure. The methods vary, but the outcome remains consistent. Quiet. Controlled. Delayed."

He inhaled slowly.

"This is not rage."

Another image appeared on the screen.

A white index card. A Latin phrase written neatly across it.

Primum non nocere.

Gasps rippled through the room.

"He leaves this behind," T'Shaka said. "Not as a message to law enforcement, but as a warning."

Someone whispered, "The Hippocratic Oath."

"Yes," T'Shaka said. "Which is why I am formally designating this offender as The Hippocratic Ghost."

The name moved through the room instantly, spreading with electric speed.

"The Ghost does not act impulsively," T'Shaka continued. "He plans extensively. He selects his targets carefully. And he genuinely believes he is ending harm the way a surgeon removes disease."

Another reporter raised her voice. "Agent Malone, how do you stop someone who believes they are right?"

T'Shaka paused.

"When someone believes they hold moral certainty," he said at last, "they expose one critical vulnerability."

The room leaned forward.

"Control," he said. "This offender's greatest strength is also his weakness. When his sense of control is threatened, when his narrative is challenged, he will accelerate. And when he accelerates, he will make mistakes."

The Director glanced at him, then returned her attention to the room.

"And make no mistake," T'Shaka added, "we are challenging that narrative now."

In Atlanta, Christy leaned forward on her bed, her jaw set.

"That's right," she muttered. "Talk to him."

Her friends were watching her more than the screen.

In Nashville, Bobby Lee nodded slowly, pride tightening in his chest.

"That boy is not guessing," he said. "He knows."

Clarence Malone said nothing, but his eyes never left the television.

In Chicago, the apartment was silent.

Dr. Booker T. Atticus Williams stood now, no longer seated.

On the screen, the young FBI agent spoke with unsettling precision, describing methods, philosophies, and patterns that felt uncomfortably familiar.

Too familiar.

Booker's mother scoffed. "That spoiled prince thinks he knows everything. What a narcissist."

Booker did not respond.

For the first time in years, something unfamiliar stirred in his chest.

Not fear.

Recognition.

On the screen, T'Shaka delivered his final statement.

"The Hippocratic Ghost believes harm must be ended," he said. "I believe harm must be understood before it can be stopped."

He looked directly into the camera.

"And now that we understand him, we will find him."

The press conference dissolved into shouted questions and flashing lights.

But somewhere beyond the reach of cameras, beyond names and narratives, the Ghost listened.

And the coin, no longer spinning freely, began to wobble.

CHAPTER EIGHT
REALITY

The television went dark.

Dr. Booker T. Atticus Williams remained standing, his hands resting lightly on the back of the chair, as if he needed the contact to stay grounded. The press conference replayed itself in his mind, not the applause, not the cameras, but the words.

Eight years.

His jaw tightened.

He had never spoken the number aloud. Never written it down. Never allowed it to exist outside his private ledger. And yet the boy, no, the agent, had found it. He had traced it back to the beginning using only patterns, absence, and logic.

Eight years ago. Chicago.

The first correction.

Booker exhaled slowly through his nose, the same way he did before an incision. But this was not an operating room, and the breath did nothing to steady him.

"You see?" Yasmine Williams said from the couch. "They always exaggerate. They are trying to make your brother appear smarter than he really is. Booker T., that child could never compare to you."

Booker did not respond.

She watched him carefully. She had spent her life reading moods—hers, his, the world's. She thought she understood everything. Still, there were moments when her son unsettled her in ways she could not explain.

“Are you alright?” she asked. “You have been quiet since that boy began speaking.”

Booker’s eyes shifted toward her.

“I am fine,” he said. His voice was even, too even.

Yasmine studied him, a creeping unease beneath her skin. She loved her son fiercely. She had protected him, shaped him, and shielded him from a world she believed had already judged him. Yet at times like this, his calm felt hollow.

She looked away first.

Booker turned toward the window. The city lights blurred into something distant and indistinct. The agent had named the philosophy. Had articulated the motive. Had even identified the weakness.

Loss of control.

Booker’s fingers curled around the edge of the chair. He grabbed his jacket.

“I am going out,” he said.

“At this hour?” Yasmine asked.

“I need air.”

She did not stop him.

The bar was dim and unremarkable, the wood worn smooth by elbows and regrets. Booker sat at the far end and ordered bourbon, neat. He took the first sip slowly, letting the burn remind him he was still in command of his body, if nothing else.

The television above the bar replayed clips from the press conference.

There he was again. T'Shaka Malone. Clear-eyed. Certain. Dangerous.

Booker watched without blinking.

He is smarter than I realized, he thought.

Then, more uncomfortably, he admitted it to himself.

He might be smarter than me.

The realization hit harder than the bourbon. Not because it was true, but because it mattered.

For years, Booker had believed himself singular. Untouchable. Necessary. He had moved ahead of consequence, ahead of recognition, ahead of anyone capable of seeing the full picture.

Until now.

He felt it then, not panic, not fear, but the unmistakable tightening of the board. The sense that the game had finally gained a worthy player.

Booker's lips curved slightly.

A smile.

Not of joy.

Of acceptance.

“So,” he murmured, lifting his glass, “you can see me.”

He drank again.

The profile was accurate, but accuracy could be used against itself. If patterns could be found, patterns could be broken. Medicine evolved. So would he.

Booker set the glass down carefully.

He would change variables. Shift methods. Select differently.

Not recklessly.

Intelligently.

Back in the apartment, Yasmine sat alone. The television remained silent, but her unease lingered. She told herself it was nothing. Brilliance always carried weight. Quiet men were often misunderstood.

Still, when she turned off the lights, she left the hallway lamp on.

Just in case.

In the bar, Booker rose, composed once more.

The challenge had been issued. For the first time in eight years, correction would require adaptation.

The coin had landed.

And it demanded movement.

CHAPTER NINE
WHY MY DADDY DON'T WANT ME?

Chicago, Illinois — Thirteen Years Earlier

Before he was a doctor. Before he was a philosophy. Before he was a correction.

Before he became Dr. Booker T. Atticus Williams, he had been just Booker T.

Five years old.

Small. Silent. Already unnervingly observant.

He sat cross-legged on the living room floor, a picture book open in his lap. Not because he needed help reading, but because the act of reading gave him order. Letters behaved. Numbers followed rules. Stories made sense in ways people did not.

His mother moved in the kitchen, her back straight, her shoulders tense. The silence that had settled over the room all afternoon weighed on him. Yasmine Williams had mastered the kind of quiet that demanded a child take responsibility for it.

"Ma?" Booker's voice was soft.

No answer.

He waited. Timing mattered. He had learned that early.

"Ma?" he tried again.

She turned slowly, wiping her hands on a towel that did not need wiping. Her face carried a decision already made.

"What is it, baby?"

Booker hesitated, then asked the question that had been building for weeks—ever since he had noticed other children being picked up by fathers who seemed real and present, not shadows.

"Why don't my daddy want me?"

The air shifted.

Yasmine crouched in front of him, close enough that he could smell her perfume—sweet, familiar, and yet misleading. Her expression softened, but behind her eyes, a sharp truth remained.

"He didn't want us," she said.

Booker blinked, trying to understand the words.

"He left," she continued, her voice calm, rehearsed, almost tender. "He went and started another family, like we never mattered."

Booker frowned, trying to piece the sentence together.

"Did I do something wrong?" he asked.

Yasmine paused, just a flicker, as if weighing the perfect lie against the perfect truth.

Then she smiled.

"No, baby," she said quickly. "You were perfect. Too good for him."

Her hand rested on his cheek, holding it a moment longer than necessary.

"He didn't want the responsibility. Men like that never do."

Booker swallowed.

At five, he could not understand betrayal, but he understood replacement.

"What if I be really good?" he asked quietly. "Will he want me then?"

Yasmine stood, her answer sharp and final.

"No. He already chose."

The conversation ended.

Booker stayed on the floor, the book slipping closed in his lap, its pages leaving only faint impressions of order.

At the same moment, in Nashville, Tennessee, Bobby Lee held his newborn daughter, Tasheema Malone-Lee, in a hospital room. His face softened in awe as she wrapped her tiny fingers around his thumb. He whispered promises he fully intended to keep.

He did not know that five-year-old boy existed in Chicago.

No letters. No calls. No truth allowed through.

Back in the apartment, Booker stared at his hands—small, capable, already steady.

If his father had left… If his father had chosen another family…

Then love was conditional. Presence was temporary. Safety had to be earned and controlled.

That night, Booker did not cry.

He lined his toys in perfect rows. He counted the cracks in the ceiling.
He listened to the rhythm of his mother's footsteps.

If people could vanish without warning, then he would become someone who never did.

Years later, the world would describe Dr. Booker T. Atticus Williams as calm. Measured. Unemotional.

They would never see the five-year-old boy whose heart cracked quietly under a lie spoken with certainty.

A boy seven years older than the brother he would never meet.

A boy who learned far too early that harm did not always announce itself loudly.

Sometimes it came softly. Wrapped in protection. And stayed forever.

CHAPTER TEN
WHO OWNS JUSTICE?

The conversation reached T'Shaka before the threats did.

It started on BET.

A roundtable. Studio lights. Smooth transitions. Familiar faces with serious reputations. The chyron below them asked the question simmering quietly for weeks:

IS DR. T'SHAKA MALONE A SELL-OUT?

The host introduced the panel with measured reverence. Dr. Cornel West leaned forward first, fingers steepled, voice calm and deliberate.

"This is a brilliant young brother operating within institutions that have historically failed our people," he said. "The question is not about his intelligence. It is about the structures he has chosen to trust." He paused, offering a knowing smile. "If I were a gambling man, I would wager that the late J. Edgar Hoover is turning over in his grave at the thought of intellect, professionalism, and the color of skin becoming the face of the FBI, an institution that has long persecuted Black bodies."

Across from him, Cousin Jeff shook his head, leaning forward with earnest conviction. "Y'all have watched this boy grow up. Since he was thirteen. Since Germany. Since Nashville. We cannot turn on him now just because he wears a badge. It is better for our community to wait and see what he produces than to condemn him for fighting in a way that looks different from what some expect."

His eyes scanned the young audience in the studio. Some seemed conflicted. Others nodded, quietly agreeing. A few appeared only to be on television, but even they seemed drawn into the discussion.

Cousin Jeff continued. “I challenge everyone here and at home to consider this: What would Malcolm X and Dr. King say if they could meet today? They disagreed, yes, but they also recognized shared principles. Ask yourselves—do you truly believe Dr. T’Shaka is a traitor to his people?”

Toure’ interjected calmly. “The concern is whether proximity to power changes outcomes or merely creates the appearance of change. History gives us reasons to be skeptical.”

Sister Souljah did not soften her words. “The system does not absorb you. It repurposes you. That is the danger. My people must always question leadership and never follow blindly.” The room seemed to hold its breath. Listening to her forced thought, reflection, whether agreement or disagreement.

At the far end, Ananda Lewis cut through the tension. “We are talking about a teenager who has been fighting for Black innocence while most of us worried about prom. Let’s not erase that.”

The debate spread quickly.

On the radio—92Q in Nashville—callers flooded the lines. Some defended T’Shaka with fierce loyalty. Others questioned his motives. A few crossed lines that should never be crossed.

It was one thing to criticize him. It was another to question his family.

T’Shaka sat alone in a quiet FBI office. The television was muted. Captions scrolled across the screen. He did not flinch at the word “sell-out.” He had lived long enough inside scrutiny to understand criticism as the cost of visibility.

But when commentators speculated about his parents, when blogs dragged Christy's name into it, when a caller laughed about "protecting him while the streets decide he picked the wrong side"—something inside him tightened.

This is not about me anymore, he thought.

Across campus in Atlanta, Christy Jones had the volume turned all the way up.

"Absolutely not," she snapped at the screen. "How could the Black community turn on T'Shaka?"

Her friends watched her closely. They recognized the look—the one that meant Christy was already calculating responses, the look of a Nubian war goddess.

"He can be questioned, but his family is off-limits. Period," she said.

Her fingers flew across the laptop. Emails drafted. Calls queued to radio stations. Receipts gathered. She did not shout. She moved.

In Nashville, Bobby Lee turned off the television with a sharp click. "That is enough," he said. "They do not get to rewrite my son."

Clarence Malone sat in his van. "The world forgets too quickly who he has been protecting."

In Chicago, Dr. Booker T. Atticus Williams watched the same clips in silence.

The irony was not lost on him.

The boy—his little brother—was accused of betrayal for believing in law.

Booker knew some might call him a monster if they understood what it meant to believe the law had already failed.

Two philosophies. Same wound.

For the first time, Booker did not feel contempt. He felt something closer to conflict.

If harm is defined by outcome, he thought, what happens when intention is clean, but consequence is not?

On BET, the final voice cut through the noise.

Louis Farrakhan appeared on screen, composed and deliberate.

"This young brother has stood for Black life when many were silent," he said. "Disagreement is not betrayal. We will not allow our children to be isolated while serving justice."

He paused.

"The Nation of Islam and the Fruit of Islam stand ready to provide security to Dr. T'Shaka Malone's family if needed. We protect our own."

The room went quiet.

Back in Quantico, T'Shaka turned the sound back on just in time to hear the words.

He closed his eyes—not in relief, but in recognition.

Support has a cost, he realized. Protection shapes the fight.

For the first time since the case began, he felt the question shift—not only professionally, but personally.

If harm is allowed by systems. If harm is corrected by force. If harm is amplified by the crowd.

Then where does responsibility truly live?

Somewhere between Atlanta, Nashville, Chicago, and the glare of national attention, two brothers—one unaware of the other's blood, the other fully aware of his brother and his plight—quietly reconsidered the same question.

The coin, now under a spotlight it never asked for, refused to stay still.

CHAPTER ELEVEN
I'M SORRY

The conference room at Quantico had no windows.

It didn't need them.

The lights hummed softly overhead, fluorescent and unforgiving, illuminating a long-polished table that had heard more secrets than most courtrooms. Director Mia Strong sat at the head, hands folded, her expression unreadable in the way only seasoned power learned to be.

T'Shaka Malone entered first. Angel Gonzales followed, closing the door behind them.

"This isn't about the Waco case," Angel said quietly, more observation than question.

"No," Director Strong replied. "It isn't."

She gestured for them to sit.

They did.

For a moment, no one spoke. Mia Strong studied T'Shaka, not the prodigy, not the headlines, not the symbol, but the young man who had walked into her office years ago with clarity instead of bravado.

"I owe you honesty," she said finally. "And an apology."

That caught his attention.

Angel's brow furrowed. "Apology for what?"

Mia exhaled, slow and controlled.

"For the assumption that talent would be enough to protect you."

She slid a thin folder across the table. T'Shaka didn't open it yet. He already felt the weight of it.

"Over the last forty-eight hours," she continued, "we've received reliable intelligence indicating concern, high-level concern, from members of the Senate."

Angel stiffened. "Concern about what?"

"About him," she said, nodding toward T'Shaka.

The word sat heavy in the room.

"Let me be clear," Mia went on. "Not concern about your conduct. Not your competence. Concern about your existence in this role."

T'Shaka finally opened the folder.

Redacted memos. Carefully worded phrases. Language designed to look procedural while bleeding fear between the lines.

Destabilizing precedent. Unpredictable influence. Threat to institutional balance.

Angel swore under his breath.

"They're scared," Angel said.

"Yes," Mia replied. "And worse, they're disappointed."

T'Shaka looked up. "Disappointed?"

Mia met his eyes. "You weren't promoted because they believed in you."

Silence.

“You were promoted,” she said, voice steady but tight, “because some people believed you would fail. Publicly. Quietly. Or catastrophically.”

Angel pushed back in his chair. “You’re saying—”

“I’m saying,” Mia interrupted, “that your appointment was supposed to be proof that the system couldn’t change. That brilliance without obedience would break.”

T’Shaka sat very still.

For the first time in his life, the shape of opposition revealed itself, not as a face, not as a voice, but as an absence. A pressure. A resistance built into the walls.

Enemies with no names. Hands with no fingerprints.

“I’m sorry,” Mia said again, softer now. “I thought proximity to excellence would force reconsideration. I underestimated how deeply some people fear disruption.”

Angel looked at T’Shaka. “You okay?”

T’Shaka nodded slowly.

“I’ve been criticized before,” he said. “I’ve been doubted. That’s not new.”

Mia tilted her head. “This is different.”

“Yes,” he agreed. “This is quieter.”

She studied him, searching for hesitation.

“What do you want to do?” she asked.

T'Shaka closed the folder and slid it back across the table.

"I want to finish the case," he said.

Angel blinked. "That's it?"

"That's everything," T'Shaka replied.

Mia leaned back, exhaling. "You understand what that means."

"Yes, ma'am."

"You'll be isolated."

"I already am."

"You'll be watched."

"I always have been."

"You'll be blamed if this goes wrong."

T'Shaka didn't flinch.

"Every meaningful thing I've done," he said calmly, "came with the expectation that I would fail. I didn't survive eighteen years by accident."

The room held him in silence.

Mia Strong nodded once.

"Then we move forward," she said. "Carefully. Quietly. And with eyes open."

Angel stood. "We've got your back."

T'Shaka rose with him.

As they reached the door, Mia spoke one last time.

“Agent Malone.”

He turned.

“Whatever happens next,” she said, “remember this: you are not alone, even when they try to make you feel like you are.”

T’Shaka gave a small nod.

Outside the conference room, the corridor stretched long and empty.

Angel clapped him on the shoulder. “Welcome to the real job.”

T’Shaka allowed himself a breath.

Enemies unseen. Systems unsettled. Truth under pressure.

This was his crucible.

And like everything else in his life over the last eighteen years, he intended to walk through it, not untouched, but unbroken.

CHAPTER TWELVE
THE KID

Agent Angel Gonzalez sat alone in his office, the door closed, the noise of Quantico fading into a low hum. A case file lay open on his desk, untouched. His reflection stared back at him from the darkened computer screen: lined face, silver threaded through black hair, eyes that had learned the cost of hesitation a long time ago.

He chuckled under his breath.

The kid.

Six months ago, the word had meant something else entirely.

Back then, Angel Gonzalez was a problem you didn't assign lightly.

At fifty-five years old, Angel Gonzalez brought a wealth of experience to the Bureau. His career with the FBI spanned fifteen years, marked by dedication and an unyielding commitment to his work. Before joining the Bureau, Angel served in the United States Army, where he was an Army Ranger—one of the most demanding and elite roles in the military. His leadership abilities led him to the position of Drill Sergeant, a role he held until his retirement after twenty years of distinguished service in the Army. These experiences shaped him into the agent he was today—disciplined, resilient, and always prepared for the challenges that lay ahead.

Dallas, Texas, raised. War tested. Scar proven.

Angel had kicked in doors in places that never made the news. He had buried friends with flags folded so tight they felt like stone. He carried himself the way men did when they'd survived long enough to stop explaining themselves.

He didn't smile on duty, not because he couldn't, but because smiles got people sloppy.

So, when the call came from upstairs, Angel already knew something was wrong.

"Agent Gonzalez," Director Mia Strong had said, voice calm in that dangerous way of hers, "we're assigning you a new partner."

Angel leaned back in his chair. "Who's the unlucky bastard?"

There had been a pause.

Then: "Dr. T'Shaka Malone."

Angel blinked. "The consultant? The kid?"

"The agent," she corrected.

Angel sat up. "Ma'am, with all due respect—"

"He's eighteen," he is ready, like dropping a live round on the table.

Angel stood.

"Please, ma'am," he said carefully, "reconsider. I cannot babysit a child."

The silence on the other end of the line was immediate, and lethal.

When Director Strong finally spoke, her voice could have frozen the sun.

"Agent Gonzalez," she said, "you will watch your tone."

Angel straightened instinctively.

"You will take Agent Malone on a ride-along," she continued. "One. You will observe. You will report back. And you will do your job."

"Yes, ma'am," Angel said, teeth clenched.

He hung up and stared at the wall.

Chaos. Pure chaos.

When he finally met the kid, Angel had expected something else. Not the calm. Not the eyes. Not the silence that wasn't empty.

T'Shaka Malone stood when Angel entered the room. Didn't rush. Didn't fidget. Didn't try to impress.

"Agent Gonzalez," the kid said. "It's an honor."

Angel grunted. "You know how to hold a firearm?"

"Yes, sir."

"You know how to take orders?"

"Yes, sir."

"You know when to shut up?"

A beat.

"Yes, sir."

Angel almost smiled.

Almost.

It wasn't until later, much later, that the ground shifted.

The gym had been Angel's idea. He needed to see what the kid did when pressure turned physical, when thought had to become instinct.

"Friendly spar," Angel had said, wrapping his hands. "Just movement."

The kid nodded.

Five minutes later, Angel was flat on his back, staring at the ceiling, lungs burning, pride bruised worse than his ribs.

The kid stood over him, breathing steady.

"You okay?" T'Shaka asked, offering a hand.

Angel stared at him.

Not a fluke. Not luck. Control.

That was when it clicked.

This wasn't a child.

This was a weapon that thought faster than it struck.

Director Strong hadn't demanded the best for the sake of optics.

She had demanded it because nothing less would survive what was coming.

Now, sitting in his office, Angel shook his head and laughed quietly.

"Kid," he muttered, this time with something like reverence.

T'Shaka Malone wasn't just brilliant. He was disciplined. Grounded. Dangerous in the right way.

Angel had seen killers with less restraint and heroes with less spine.

He closed the file and stood.

When Angel Gonzalez called T'Shaka, "Kid," now, it wasn't dismissal.

It was acknowledgment.

It meant: I see you. It meant: You're one of mine.

And if the world thought an eighteen-year-old couldn't walk into the fire, Angel Gonzalez knew better, then it will learn as he did and many others whoever doubted Agent T'Shaka Malone.

He'd already seen the kid step in and make the flames behave.

CHAPTER THIRTEEN
THE TREE

December 13,1999.

The movie was bad.

Not fun-bad. Just bad.

The kind of Christmas horror film that forces you to yell at the screen because the girl keeps sprinting upstairs instead of out the damn door. *Silent Night, Deadly Night* flickered across the television in Bobby Lee Malone's living room. Snow fell softly outside. Inside, the house glowed warm with laughter and the easy rhythm of family.

"Why would she do that?" Christy groaned, half-laughing, half-annoyed.

T'Shaka shook his head, a soft smile spreading across his face as he leaned closer to Christy. He pressed a gentle kiss to her neck, lingering on the spot he knew was especially sensitive to his touch. For a moment, he allowed himself to lose focus on everything else, letting the warmth and familiarity of Christy's presence envelop him, her perfume Gucci Rush, made him lose control. The world outside faded away as he concentrated on the intimacy they shared—his attention drawn entirely to her, and the quiet comfort between them.

They were curled together on the couch, legs tangled, comfortable in the deep, quiet way that comes from knowing someone. Nashville felt quiet that night. Safe. Normal.

Then the pager vibrated.

Once.

Sharp. Unmistakable.

T'Shaka froze, "Dammit!"

Christy giggled, she didn't need to ask what it was. She already knew.

"That's Director Strong," she said softly.

He nodded, stood, already reaching for the phone. The kiss they shared before he stepped away was brief, but heavy with everything unsaid.

"Ma'am" he answered when the line connected.

Her voice came through steady, stripped clean of warmth.

"We need you in Mississippi," she said. "Immediately."

His stomach tightened. "What happened?"

"A young man. African American. College student. Found hanging from a tree outside Meridian."

The word *hanging* landed like a physical blow.

"What's his name?" T'Shaka asked.

"Omar Wells Jr.," she replied. "Freshman at Ole Miss. Home for Christmas break. Body discovered twenty miles from Meridian College."

T'Shaka closed his eyes.

"Yes," he said. "I'm on my way."

Christy was already in his room packing, she refused to let T'Shaka be alone during the holidays.

T'Shaka smiled as he overheard Christy on the phone with her mother, explaining that she would be accompanying him to Mississippi. Though her mother's voice carried a note of disappointment, she ultimately understood Christy's decision—she, too, did not want T'Shaka to face this alone.

Next Day Mississippi

Director Strong pulled them off the Hippocratic Ghost case without hesitation.

Some cases demanded speed. Others demanded precision. This one demanded reverence.

By the time T'Shaka and Agent Angel Gonzalez arrived in Mississippi, word had spread like fire through dry grass. Squad cars lined the dirt road. Local deputies stood back—uneasy, some curious, some defensive.

And some afraid.

T'Shaka stepped out of the vehicle slowly.

He wore a black-and-silver Malcolm X, long sleeve sweater beneath a heavy peacoat, collar turned up against the cold. Blue jeans. Black-and-red Jordan 5s already dusted with Mississippi red clay. Around his neck hung a fourteen-karat gold chain with a small medallion—his grandfather Clarence Malone's picture, visible only if you were looking for it, accompanied by his FBI badge.

Angel noticed. So did everyone else.

The tree stood ahead of them—old, thick, rooted deep and unyielding into the earth. Omar Wells Jr.,18 years of age; his body hung in the tree, the scene had long silenced after the horror that transpired, violence still clung to the air. The ground beneath the branches was churned. A faint horizontal scar marked the bark. Fibers snagged where they had no business being.

T'Shaka didn't rush.

He never did.

He circled the tree and the body once. Twice. Looked up into the branches, then down at the soil.

"Height?" he asked quietly.

"About eighteen feet," a local deputy answered.

T'Shaka nodded. "That matters."

He crouched, studying the ground—not touching anything, just reading with his eyes. Drag marks. Uneven pressure points. A break in the grass pattern that spoke of multiple bodies moving.

"This wasn't a suicide," someone muttered nearby.

T'Shaka didn't respond. He already knew.

He stepped back, closed his eyes for a single breath, then began to speak—not loudly, but clearly enough that every person present leaned in.

"Omar Wells Jr. did not climb this tree," he said. "He was brought here."

Angel crossed his arms. "Walk us through it, kid."

T'Shaka opened his eyes.

"The ligature marks show postmortem suspension," he explained. "The pressure pattern indicates the body was lifted, not dropped from a jump. No panic abrasions on the hands or forearms. No bark under the nails."

He pointed to the soil.

"Drag marks show the body was moved twelve to fifteen feet from the point of initial contact. Multiple individuals were involved. At least three."

One of the deputies shifted his weight, uncomfortable as he decided to check the distance, Dr. Malone was correct.

"This wasn't about killing him quickly," T'Shaka continued. "This was about display."

The word hung heavy in the cold air.

"This location is deliberate," he said. "Visible, but not immediate. Close enough to be discovered. Far enough to send a message."

Angel exhaled slowly. "Lynching."

"Yes," T'Shaka said. "But not impulsive."

He turned, eyes sharp now.

"This is performative violence," he said. "Designed to reclaim narrative control. Someone wanted to remind this community of fear. Of hierarchy. Of history."

Silence swallowed the scene.

"This is not the work of a lone actor," he added. "And it is not random."

Angel nodded once. "Profile?"

T'Shaka didn't pause.

"Offenders are local," he said. "They feel protected by familiarity. Likely male. Likely organized through shared grievance—economic, racial, ideological. They expected leniency in case they were caught."

He let the words settle.

"They did not expect me."

The air changed.

Christy sat at the edge of the bed watching the local news in Meridian and T'Shaka speak at the crime scene, arms folded, eyes burning. She had seen T'Shaka angry before—but this was different. This was focused. Controlled. Purposeful.

This wasn't just a case.

This was history knocking again.

And T'Shaka Malone had no intention of letting the door stay open.

CHAPTER FOURTEEN
OMAR

The drive was quiet.

Mississippi roads stretched long and narrow, framed by trees that seemed older than memory. As the vehicle slowed near a small cluster of businesses outside Meridian, T'Shaka's eyes shifted, not wandering, but cataloging.

"Stop," he said calmly.

Angel Gonzalez eased the car to the shoulder without asking why.

Across the road sat a pawn shop. Weathered. Functional. Ordinary, until it wasn't.

A rebel flag hung in the front window, faded but deliberate. Beneath it, a hand-painted sign read:

SONS OF THUNDER

The lettering was jagged. Aggressive. Fresh.

"Aryan," Angel muttered.

"Yes," T'Shaka replied. "And small. Upstart."

Angel glanced at him. "You're sure?"

T'Shaka considered the scene, his expression steady. "They advertise," he observed, his tone low but certain. "People with real power don't need to put themselves on display like that." He paused, then continued, "I read up on them—and on several other white-militia groups in the area—while we were on the plane ride here."

Agent Gonzo thought to himself, The Kid will never be caught unprepared.

They rolled forward again, the image burned into T'Shaka's mind, not emotionally, but structurally. He logged the distance calculating distance and time. The angles. The surrounding roads.

Six miles later, another detail surfaced.

A gas station and tire shop. One pump out of order. A dumpster overflowing near the back. And tied loosely to a broken fence, a strip of red cloth fluttered in the cold wind.

T'Shaka's gaze sharpened.

The red wasn't random.

It carried a pattern; a crude lightning bolt motif stitched into the fabric.

The same pattern as the lettering on the Sons of Thunder sign.

Angel caught it too.

"Six miles," Angel said quietly. "You thinking transport?"

"Yes," T'Shaka replied. "And struggle."

They reached the perimeter of the crime scene moments later.

The ground near the tree told a story no one else had bothered to read yet.

Deep tire impressions. Wide. Heavy. Truck, likely lifted.

"Tread depth suggests aftermarket tires," T'Shaka said, stepping carefully around the marks. "Not factory. Someone proud of the look."

Angel nodded. "Same kind of guys who hang flags."

T'Shaka crouched near a patch of disturbed soil. There, caught in the roots, another fragment of red fabric. Torn. Stretched. Pulled free with force.

"Omar fought," T'Shaka said softly.

Angel didn't respond immediately.

He didn't need to.

T'Shaka stood, eyes distant now, not lost, but assembling something larger than the scene itself. A sequence. A timeline.

He turned to Angel.

"You already see it, don't you?" T'Shaka asked.

Angel smirked faintly. "Yes, kid."

The word didn't sting anymore.

It grounded.

T'Shaka smiled, just a fraction.

"Gonzo," he said, voice shifting into focus mode, "we need to see Omar's body again."

Angel raised an eyebrow. "You thinking postmortem trace?"

"Yes," T'Shaka replied. "If I'm correct, there will be fabric fibers under his nails, red, synthetic blend. Likely acrylic or nylon."

"And chemicals?" Angel asked.

"Fuel residue," T'Shaka said. "Diesel or industrial lubricant. Something consistent with a gas station/tire shop environment. He grabbed at whoever restrained him."

Angel nodded once. "And DNA."

"Yes," T'Shaka said. "Omar left us a map. We just have to read it."

They stood there for a moment longer, the weight of the place pressing in.

This wasn't just about catching killers.

This was about honoring resistance.

Omar Wells Jr. had not gone quietly.

And Dr. T'Shaka Malone intended to make sure the world knew it.

The hotel room was quiet in the way only grief could make it.

The television was off. The curtains were half-drawn. Outside, Mississippi night pressed heavy against the glass, humid and unmoving. T'Shaka sat on the edge of the bed, elbows on his knees, hands clasped so tightly his knuckles had gone pale.

He looked older now.

Not just tired, weathered.

Eighteen years hadn't prepared him for this kind of weight. The kind that didn't challenge the mind but hollowed out the chest. The kind that didn't ask for answers, only endurance.

Christy watched him from across the room.

She had seen him brilliant. She had seen him calm. She had seen him unshakable.

This was different.

She crossed the room slowly, careful not to rush the moment, and stood in front of him. For a second, she just looked at him, really looked. The boy she had known since first grade. The genius the world claimed. The man everyone leaned on.

Her voice softened.

“Aw, T’Shaka Malone…”

It wasn’t teasing. It wasn’t playful.

It was permission.

Something inside him broke open.

T’Shaka reflected on his trip to the Wells home.

Flashback earlier after the gas station:

T’Shaka turned to Gonzo, hey partner we need to go by Omar Wells Jr. family home.

Gonzo wasn’t against that, it was normal, but this case seems to already be a heavy task, not because of the case but what the case represent. And Gonzo knew that T’Shaka carried the weight of his people, much like Gonzalez had done in the past and what he still continues to carry.

Gonzalez did only what a good partner could do, support him and pull him back when things become too heavy.

Thirty minutes later Gonzalez and T'Shaka arrived at the Wells' family home. The house was a nice size built for need rather than comfort. A tall dark-skinned man stood out front, he was wearing an Ole Miss hat, proud of his son's accomplishment. Followed by a short woman wearing a dress, with a white apron, and house shoes.

T'Shaka and Gonzalez learned that it was Omar's mother, Mrs. Betty Wells, a school teacher who at some point taught every child and she was the music director.

Omar Wells Sr, who was often called Big Omar after the birth of his son Jr., was a stand offish at first but then softened up after his wife whispered in his ear. Omar's sisters, little brother, and other kin was present, the house had white wall paper with blue flowers, neatly done, the floor was hand crafted hardwood, the kitchen smelled good, the fragrance from the greens said, "welcome."

The family room had a black piano, I was told by Ms. Kimberly, Omar's aunt who was four years older than him that the piano was custom built by their great grandfather who fixed pianos and who belonged to a gospel quartet, that same quartet known as the Meridian Five, raised money for the local church.

As the agents sat in the living room, drinking home made fruit tea, Omar Wells Sr, spoke, "They killed my boy... His voice cracked, and for the first time T'Shaka saw a man of strength, honor, stubborn, and always viewed as the protector... He broke down and said, "Please Dr. Malone, get them evil men, who killed my boy... my boy."

For some reason T'Shaka eyes became fixated on a wooden plaque below a Black Jesus painting:

Matthew 11:28-30; Come to me, all you who are weary and burdened, and I will give you rest. Take my yoke upon you and learn from me, for I am gentle and humble in heart, and you will find rest for your souls. For my yoke is easy and my burden is light."

T'Shaka was never religious, and he often wrestled with faith especially as it relates to the suffering of Black folks, but for some reason that plaque angered him and yet it centered him in this moment. Until Omar's older sister who was the same age as his aunt, Stephanie spoke: "Dr. Malone… I don't know if you ever knew this," she began, her hands twisting together in her lap, knuckles pale.

"Omar always said he was going to be an engineer. Since he was little. He used to take apart anything he could get his hands on—radios, remotes, even the church microphone once."

A faint smile flickered across her face, then disappeared.

"He said he wanted to build bridges. Said bridges brought people together."

Her voice cracked.

"But then… he saw you."

The room stilled.

"He saw that story about a Black boy his age solving a crime all the way in Germany. A Black boy who didn't leave Nashville but still changed the world. And when they put that Nobel Peace Prize around your neck…"

She stopped. Drew a shaky breath.

"He stood right there in this living room. Pointed at the television. And he said, 'Momma… he look like me.'"

Her tears came now, quiet but unstoppable.

"And then he said, 'Momma, I'm going to be like T'Shaka Malone. I'm going to save people. I'm going to solve cases just like him.'"

Her voice lowered to almost a whisper.

"He stopped talking about bridges after that."

A beat.

"And one night before bed, he told me, 'Don't worry, Momma. One day me and T'Shaka gonna be partners. We gonna fix things together.'"

She covered her mouth, the weight finally too much.

"He believed in you, Dr. Malone. The way little boys believe in superheroes."

Silence fell.

Not just grief.

Responsibility.

Gonzalez glanced at his partner.

T'Shaka stood straight, hands folded in front of him, composed as ever.

But his eyes were red.

Not from weakness.

From restraint.

Mrs. Betty Wells saw it immediately.

And in that quiet exchange, she understood what so many Black mothers understand without explanation — that brilliance does not shield a young Black man from grief. That strength does not cancel sorrow. That even the strong need covering.

She said nothing.

She simply nodded at him, as if to say, *I see you, son.*

After dinner, the Wells family gathered in the living room.

The television went dark.

Plates were stacked.

And without instruction, they began to sing.

"Grace and Mercy…"

The first voice was soft.

Then another joined.

Then harmony.

No instruments. No polish.

Just history in melody.

T'Shaka shifted his weight. He wasn't uncomfortable — he was analytical. Observing.

He did not believe in divine intervention. He believed in causality. In policy. In reform.

Grace, to him, was systemic leniency.

Mercy was judicial discretion.

But as Mrs. Wells' voice trembled on the word *grace*, something unsettled him.

Because grace, in that room, was not legal.

It was unearned.

And that contradicted everything he believed about balance.

He felt his chest tighten.

If grace exists, he thought, *then what is justice?*

Across the room, Gonzalez lowered his head.

Subtle. Almost instinctive.

His thumb brushed the small cross resting beneath his shirt collar — a habit he hadn't practiced openly since his Army days.

He didn't analyze the lyrics.

He absorbed them.

His grandmother used to sing that same hymn in Spanish, voice cracked with age, incense thick in the air.

He understood mercy differently.

To him, mercy was not weakness.

It was the thing that kept men from becoming what they hunted.

Gonzalez opened his eyes and glanced at T'Shaka.

He could see the tension in his partner's jaw.

The battle wasn't visible — but it was happening.

T'Shaka wasn't moved by the music.

He was disturbed by it.

Because the hymn suggested something dangerous:

That Omar's killer might need mercy.

And T'Shaka did not know if he could accept a world where mercy applied to men who weaponized harm.

The children's voices rose stronger on the final refrain.

"Your grace and mercy brought me through..."

T'Shaka's vision blurred for just a moment.

Not from faith.

From the possibility that justice alone might not be enough.

The song ended.

Silence lingered.

Not awkward.

Reverent.

And for the first time since Omar's body was found, T'Shaka felt something he could not categorize.

Not anger.

Not resolve.

Something heavier.

Something spiritual.

The car ride back to the hotel was quiet, not awkward but two men working out the complexities that this case and life offered.

As they got out of the car Gonzelz called out: “Hey Kid, I got your back.”

T’Shaka smiled, “I know old man.”

Nothing else needed to be said because this partnership was being formed in the midst of a crucible.

Flashback ends.

Christy covered her mouth at what she heard.

T’Shaka stood suddenly, six feet of discipline and restraint, and folded into her as if gravity had finally given up on him. Christy wrapped her arms around him without hesitation, anchoring him, holding him the way she always had when the world asked too much.

For the first time since Mississippi, T’Shaka allowed himself to be human.

Not an agent. Not a symbol. Not a prodigy.

A son. A brother. A cousin. A young Black man trying to understand how a sin could continue to sin without conscience.

His shoulders shook.

“Omar Jr…” he whispered.

Christy tightened her hold, resting her cheek against his chest. She didn’t try to quiet him. She didn’t try to fix it.

She just stayed.

He cried the name again.

"Omar Jr…"

It wasn't just grief for a life taken, it was rage restrained, love unspent, history repeating itself with cruel familiarity. It was the burden of knowing that justice, for his people, always arrived late and paid in blood.

Christy felt it all.

"This isn't on you," she whispered, even though she knew he wouldn't fully believe it. "But you're going to make it right."

He nodded against her hair, breath uneven.

She kissed his forhead gently. Don't think too much just do it."

"You always find a way my T'Shaka Malone."

They stood there for a long moment, the world outside forgotten.

This was their rhythm.

Christy, fire and protection. T'Shaka, thought and restraint.

Together, they made space for survival.

And as the night deepened, one truth settled unmistakably in the room:

T'Shaka Malone didn't just represent justice.

He carried it.

And the cost of carrying it was never paid alone.

CHAPTER FIFTEEN
A SECOND WIND

In track and field, every runner knows about the second wind.

It isn't myth. It isn't luck. It's science sharpened by discipline.

The second wind comes when the body should fail but doesn't. When patience holds long enough for endurance to turn into momentum. When suffering gives way to clarity.

For T'Shaka Malone, the second wind arrived just before dawn.

Christy woke that dinner that the Wells sent with T'Shaka was devoured and it put out her light. Christ found T'Shaka sitting upright on the edge of the bed, back straight, shoulders squared, eyes dark and focused. Not tired. Not frantic.

Resolved.

She didn't need to ask.

He had that look—the one she'd learned to recognize since childhood. The look that meant his mind had moved past pain and into purpose.

On the small desk beside him lay maps, handwritten notes, a rough grid of roads and properties within a twenty-mile radius. He had already circled three locations, all tied to proximity, ideology, and access to vehicles.

"Sons of Thunder," he murmured. "They don't hide far from where they work, they are bold and believe themselves outside of the law."

Christy stretched and leaned against the headboard, watching him. Just then, the pager went off.

Lab results.

T'Shaka didn't flinch. He reached for the phone calmly, already knowing what it would confirm.

Christy crossed the room and kissed him softly.

"I knew it," she said. "You got your second wind."

He smiled faintly. "I Always do baby."

To T'Shaka, it was a gift born from two things he had mastered early: dislike and patience. Dislike for injustice. Patience enough to outlast it.

Christy smiled back, dimples flashing, white teeth bright even in the early light. To him, she was the most beautiful woman in the world—not because of how she looked, but because she understood him when everyone else called him that weird kid.

"Keep your gun close today," he said gently. "You'll be escorted to the Wells house. Family stays together."

She nodded. "I know."

"I don't trust anyone," he added quietly, "who isn't in my circle or who doesn't look like me."

She didn't argue.

She never did.

By the time T'Shaka arrived at the local FBI field office, the fax machine was already humming.

The lab results confirmed everything.

Red synthetic fibers—nylon-acrylic blend. Diesel residue. Industrial lubricant. Multiple DNA profiles beneath Omar Wells Jr.'s fingernails.

And a match.

A search warrant had already been transmitted—first to the gas station six miles out, then directly to John Russell, registered owner and operator.

Reinforcements were en route.

The net was tightening.

That was when Deputy Dewey Jacobs stepped into his path.

Jacobs was mid-forties. Red-faced. Smiling in the wrong way.

"Look here, boy," he drawled. "Shame what happened to that Wells kid. Real shame he went and committed suicide."

T'Shaka laughed.

Not loudly. Not cruelly.

Just enough.

Jacobs frowned. "What's funny?"

T'Shaka held up the folder in his hand. "You are."

Jacobs bristled. "Excuse me?"

"You're talking about suicide," T'Shaka said calmly, "while I'm holding forensic proof of homicide. And while a search warrant is already being executed."

Jacobs' smile slipped.

Agent Gonzalez appeared at T'Shaka's side like gravity itself.

"You will refer to my partner as Agent Malone," Gonzalez said coldly, "or Dr. Malone."

Jacobs scoffed. "Or what?"

Gonzalez leaned in, voice low and lethal.

"Or you'll shut up and get out of the way before you embarrass yourself further."

Jacobs opened his mouth.

Gonzalez cut him off. "Actually—scratch that. You already have."

Jacobs backed away, face flushed with something that looked a lot like fear.

T'Shaka watched him go.

Now he had a face. Now he had intent. Now he had momentum.

The second wind wasn't just about endurance.

It was about closing distance.

And Dr. T'Shaka Malone was no longer running to survive.

He was running to finish.

CHAPTER SIXTEEN
TEAM GONZO AND KID

The room fell quiet the moment they entered.

U.S. Marshals, FBI tactical units, maps spread across the table, coffee gone cold. Everyone felt it, this was the pivot point.

Agent Angel Gonzalez didn't waste time.

He stepped to the podium, posture straight, voice carrying the authority of a man who had led soldiers through worse than this.

"Alright, ladies and gentlemen," Gonzo said. "Listen up."

The room leaned in.

"We're dividing into three teams: Alpha, Bravo, and Charlie."

He pointed to the map.

"Alpha, that's myself and the Kid. We hit the gas station. We serve the warrant. We dig. We don't rush, but we don't miss anything."

His finger moved.

"Bravo, you surround the Russell plantation. Surveillance only. I want pictures of everything. Mailman, dogs, vehicles, anyone who breathes near that property. No contact unless they force it. If there's hostility, you respond, but you wait for the word from me or the Kid."

A pause.

"Charlie, you stage at the crime scene. That location sits between two compounds. You're reserve. You move only if we call it."

Silence.

Then, firmly: “Any questions?”

No one spoke.

“Good,” Gonzo said. “Gear up.”

T’Shaka moved with quiet precision.

Short-sleeve polo, FBI vest snug, blue jeans, black Nike ACG hiking boots grounded and ready. He sheathed his Bowie knife across his lower back at a diagonal, smooth draw, no wasted motion. Springfield Armory 1911 seated, custom Heckler and Koch MP5A3 secured, balanced like an extension of his arm.

Georgetown Hoyas cap turned backward. With his Oakley shades on. Fingerless gloves tight. FBI windbreaker zipped halfway.

Gonzo glanced over and smirked. “Don’t you look ravishing.”

T’Shaka smiled once. “Focus, old man.”

They moved.

Black Suburban out front, engines low. The convoy rolled through the back roads like a shadow, tires eating up red dirt and pine needles. No sirens, no drama.

Until there was.

The gas station came into view, quiet, deceptively ordinary. Rusted pumps, flickering sign, the same place T’Shaka had marked hours earlier.

They exited the vehicle.

T’Shaka stepped forward, warrant folder in hand.

"Federal Bureau of Investigation," he said clearly. "We have a search—"

The gunshot cracked the air. It missed him by inches.

Instinct took over.

T'Shaka dropped, rolled, came up firing in one smooth motion. The shooter, a young man with wild eyes and a rifle too big for his frame, fell backward, struck clean between the eyes.

The name would come later. The chaos arrived immediately.

Gunfire erupted from the treeline, from behind the station, from a side door that burst open under pressure. Alpha team scattered, disciplined, controlled.

"Contact right!" Gonzo shouted.

T'Shaka was already moving.

He covered the flank, firing short, precise bursts, not wild, not panicked. Every step calculated, every shot purposeful. Gonzo moved like a tank, steady, relentless, laying down suppressive fire while shouting commands that cut through the noise.

"Charlie, hold!" Gonzo barked into the radio. "Bravo, they're running!"

The swamp swallowed them.

Six figures bolted into the tree line, splashing through water thick with reeds and mud. The ground turned treacherous, every step a gamble.

"Split," T'Shaka said calmly. "They'll fan out."

Gonzo nodded. "You take east. I'll push west."

They moved.

The swamp fought back, branches clawed, water dragged, insects screamed. But fear slowed the men running, not the ones hunting.

A suspect slipped, weapon sinking into the muck. T'Shaka was on him in seconds, knee to the back, rifle kicked away, cuffs on before the man could beg.

Another turned, fired blindly. Gonzo closed distance fast, struck the rifle aside, dropped the man with a brutal, efficient blow.

Shots echoed, shouts, then silence.

Thirteen dead.

Six captured alive, soaked, shaking, dragged out of the swamp in cuffs.

Reinforcements arrived to secure the scene. The gas station was sealed, evidence logged, the Russell network exposed.

T'Shaka stood still for a moment, chest rising, eyes scanning.

Gonzo walked up beside him, clapped a heavy hand on his shoulder.

"Good work, kid."

T'Shaka nodded, gaze steady.

This wasn't victory.

It was traction.

And now, the ground beneath them was finally moving in the right direction.

CHAPTER SEVENTEEN
THE MASK COMES OFF

Two things happened almost simultaneously.

And together, they changed everything.

John Russell was not a subtle man.

When the news broke—local channels looping shaky footage of law enforcement vehicles swarming the gas station—he sat in the shadowed back room of the Russell plantation house, boots propped on the table, a glass of bourbon sweating in his thick fingers.

The reporter's voice sliced through the quiet.

"...one suspect deceased after exchanging gunfire with federal agents. Authorities have confirmed the individual as the youngest of the seven Russell brothers..."

John surged to his feet so violently the chair crashed against the wall.

"What?" he barked.

Then the name.

Then the phrase that narrowed his world to a burning point.

"...shot by an eighteen-year-old FBI agent..."

The glass flew from his hand and exploded against the stone fireplace in a spray of amber and shards.

"That pompous Black FBI kid," he snarled, voice low and venomous.

Rage rose in him—hot, reckless, ancestral. This was not mere loss. This was humiliation. Public exposure. A direct insult to the order he believed the world still owed him.

He snatched the phone.

"Call them," he ordered. "All of them. Sons of Thunder—full mobilization. Now."

Across the county, militia compounds began to hum with movement.

Then the second call came.

This one stole the blood from his face.

"Sir," the voice said, careful, almost apologetic, "feds are at your house."

John froze. "At my—"

"They've got warrants. Everywhere. Basement, outbuildings, vehicles."

For the first time in years, something close to panic clawed at his chest.

Minutes later the flood arrived, unstoppable.

Drugs—stockpiled, packaged, ready for the streets. Illegal weapons—automatic rifles, explosives, silencers. Photographs—printed, framed, carefully hidden.

And worse.

Video.

Crystal-clear footage of Omar Wells Jr. hanging from the tree. Multiple angles. Smiling faces behind the lens.

The mask was gone.

And then the detail that finally cracked something inside him.

“That FBI kid’s girlfriend,” the voice continued. “She’s not at the Econo Lodge anymore. She’s at the Wells home.”

John’s mouth twisted into something feral, dangerous.

Back at the gas station, truth was clawing its way out of the dirt.

A garage door had been forced open. Beneath a tarp stiff with old mud sat a truck. The tires were unmistakable—thick, aggressive tread still caked with the same red clay and organic matter lifted from the lynching site.

The vehicle had not been cleaned.

They had never expected anyone to look.

Weapons lined the walls—unregistered, modified, waiting.

And then the book.

Black cover. Handwritten pages.

Names. Addresses. Family trees. Church memberships. Dates. Plans.

Agent Gonzalez stared at the open pages, jaw locked tight.

“This wasn’t random,” he said quietly.

T'Shaka stood motionless, reading without touching.

"No," he answered. "This was strategy."

The book was not only hate.

It was economics.

Land seizures. Forced displacement. Pressure campaigns. Violence dressed as fear to drive families off property their ancestors had held for generations.

At the heart of it all stood Mt. Bethel Community Church.

The pastor had refused to sell.

That refusal had choked a development pipeline—gentrification, profit, progress measured in dollars.

The church was not merely a building.

It was an obstacle.

Omar Wells Jr. had been a message.

"This wasn't about one boy," Gonzo said.

"No," T'Shaka replied. "It was about many."

He lifted his eyes, sharp, unyielding.

"They planned chaos," he said. "They planned to make the land cheap. To make the people leave. To erase an entire community."

Gonzo exhaled slowly. "And we just kicked the door in."

T'Shaka nodded once.

“Yes,” he said. “We did.”

Outside, sirens rose and fell, phones rang without pause, units surged forward.

The Sons of Thunder were no longer hidden.

They were cornered.

And in that corner—furious, humiliated, heavily armed—John Russell was already preparing to set the world on fire.

But it was already too late.

Dr. T’Shaka Malone and Agent Angel Gonzalez had done far more than solve a murder.

They had torn open a war.

And now the whole world could see it.

CHAPTER EIGHTEEN CALLING ALL SONS OF THUNDER

John Russell stood at the center of the compound, phone pressed to his ear, fury making his hands tremble.

"Calling all Sons of Thunder," he barked into the line. "It's time. Bring them hell. Bring chaos. This is—"

A voice cut through the loudspeakers before he could finish.

Calm. Young. Commanding.

"John Russell."

The entire compound went still.

John's lips curled into a slow, ugly grin as he lowered the phone. "Well, I'll be damned," he laughed. "FBI didn't even give us time to strike."

The men around him shifted uneasily, fingers tightening on rifles and shotguns.

"This," John shouted to his followers, voice rising with desperate conviction, "is a fight for white survival."

T'Shaka's POV

The night air hung thick and heavy, pressing against his skin like a held breath.

Floodlights bathed the compound in merciless white. Armored vehicles formed an unbroken ring of steel. FBI agents, U.S. Marshals, state police, tactical teams—all silent, all ready.

T'Shaka stood beside the command vehicle, megaphone steady in his grip.

He understood exactly what his presence represented to men like John Russell.

A Black man giving orders. A Black man with federal authority. A Black man who showed no fear.

And for Omar Wells Jr., he let that truth burn fully inside him.

"John Russell," T'Shaka said, voice level and clear, "you are surrounded. You have six minutes to exit the compound with your hands raised. All individuals inside are ordered to drop their weapons, lie face down, and surrender peacefully."

He paused deliberately, letting the silence stretch.

John's laughter exploded again, harsh and mocking. "You hear that, boys? The FBI sent a kid to read us bedtime stories."

T'Shaka ignored the bait. He shifted tone, voice now edged with steel.

"John Russell," he continued, "for the murder of Omar Wells Jr., for possession of illegal narcotics, for illegal firearms, and for involvement in sex trafficking, you are hereby advised of your Miranda rights."

He recited them word for word, calm and precise.

It was procedure.

It was also deliberate psychological pressure.

Because T'Shaka was prepared for whatever came next.

John's laughter died abruptly.

Then his voice returned, low and dripping venom.

"Fuck you, nigger," he spat over the open channel. "And all the nigger lovers standing with you. And by the way—your girlfriend should be dead any minute now."

The night seemed to tighten.

T'Shaka exhaled slowly through his nose.

Then he smiled, small and cold.

"Oh no," he said dryly. "You mean the men you sent to kill her?"

Dead silence on the other end.

"They're all dead," T'Shaka continued, voice flat and final. "Including your other two younger brothers."

He let the count sink in.

"That makes three brothers gone now, John. You're the last one standing."

Whispers spread through the compound like wind through dry grass—fear, doubt, fracture.

"And your sisters?" T'Shaka added quietly. "They're already in federal custody."

John's breathing rasped harshly over the speakers.

T'Shaka's voice dropped lower, each word a hammer.

"One more thing. All your assets—financial accounts, real property—have been seized. Every dollar. Every acre. Even your grandfather's plantation."

The word *plantation* landed like a physical blow.

Something inside John Russell shattered.

Not the men. Not the weapons.

His certainty. His myth. His entire world of inherited power.

There would be no legacy left to defend. No land to pass down. No future to claim.

Only consequences.

The six minutes were nearly gone.

For the first time in his life, John Russell understood he was no longer summoning an army.

He was alone.

And Dr. T'Shaka Malone—standing calm, unflinching, unbreakable—had brought the storm straight to his door.

CHAPTER NINETEEN FLASHBACK: CHRISTY AND THE WELLS

T'Shaka had planned for the worst. He always did.

He understood something most people didn't—or refused to accept: a cornered dog doesn't retreat. It bites. And men who build their lives on hate behave no differently when the world closes in.

So, he set a trap.

FLASHBACK — MERIDIAN, MISSISSIPPI (EARLIER THAT NIGHT)

Christy sat at the Wells' dining table in the soft glow of a single overhead lamp; hands wrapped around a mug of tea that had long gone cold. The house was full of life—family members, cousins, church sisters and brothers rotating in and out with quiet hugs, murmured prayers, plates of food no one really touched. But beneath the surface warmth, the air felt thick, tight with the kind of worry that settles in bones.

She felt it before anyone spoke the words.

A shift in the atmosphere. A sudden stillness in the conversations. Something coming.

Outside the quiet neighborhood, four pickup trucks roared down the narrow county road toward Mount Bethel Community Church. Confederate flags fluttered from tailgates. Sons of Thunder insignias had been spray-painted across doors and hoods in crude white letters. Men stood in the beds, rifles raised high, faces twisted with adrenaline-fueled bravado, believing they were reclaiming control, bringing terror back where they thought it belonged.

They had no idea they were driving straight into a trap.

At the final bend before the church property line, U.S. Marshals emerged from concealment—dark figures rising from ditches, tree lines, parked vehicles. Spike strips snapped across the asphalt with a metallic clatter.

The sound came first—tires screaming in protest, rubber shredding, metal grinding against metal as the lead truck hit the strips and fishtailed wildly. The second truck plowed into it, then the third, fourth—a brutal domino collapse of steel and glass. Bodies were thrown from the beds, weapons spinning into the dark grass, headlights slashing the night in frantic arcs.

Chaos erupted in seconds.

Commands cut through the roar, sharp and unrelenting.

"DROP YOUR WEAPONS!" "ON THE GROUND! NOW!" "HANDS WHERE WE CAN SEE THEM!"

Some men complied instantly—dropping rifles, falling to their knees, faces pressed to the cold, gritty road.

Others refused.

Gunfire cracked—short, controlled bursts from trained teams. No wild spraying. No hesitation. Those who raised weapons or lunged died where they stood. No dramatic last stands. No heroic speeches. Just bodies scattered across a road they had hoped to turn into a symbol of fear.

The night reclaimed its silence.

This night would not belong to them.

It belonged to reckoning.

CUT BACK — PRESENT

T'Shaka stood behind the command vehicle, megaphone steady in his right hand, eyes fixed on the brightly lit compound gates.

The clock ticked down.

One minute remaining.

Floodlights burned mercilessly, turning every shadow into stark relief. Helicopters thrummed low overhead, rotors chopping the air. The perimeter held firm—agents, marshals, state troopers, tactical units locked in position, weapons ready but disciplined.

He allowed himself one brief thought of Christy—safe inside the Wells home, surrounded by family and protected by the very team he had positioned there. He thought of the Wells family gathered around her, of Omar's photo on the mantel, of a small church that still stood because one pastor had refused to sell his soul for a quick dollar.

John Russell's voice crackled over the open channel one last time—ragged, broken, stripped of its former swagger.

But T'Shaka didn't respond.

He didn't need to.

The trap had already closed.

And when the final second vanished from the countdown, so did the last illusion that hate could ever outrun consequence.

The compound lights flickered once, as if the building itself understood surrender was the only path left.

CHAPTER TWENTY
BY ANY MEANS NECESSARY

Time expired on John Russell.

T'Shaka had already traded the megaphone for night-vision goggles. The world shifted into green-tinted clarity, edges sharpened, heat signatures glowed softly, movement slowed into deliberate, meaningful shapes. The six minutes had never been for intimidation. They had been for calculation, for patience, for ensuring that everyone who came out of this compound went home the way they arrived.

Alive.

GONZO POV

Angel Gonzalez watched the Kid tighten the strap on his goggles and felt something warm settle deep in his chest, pride mixed with quiet awe.

He thought about the first day. About how wrong he'd been. About the partner he'd lost years ago and the wall he'd built after that funeral. He smiled now, small and private, because these agents thought they had already seen what the "Kid" could do.

They hadn't.

They were about to watch the most dangerous mind in the Bureau organize chaos into order.

Gonzo leaned in as T'Shaka stepped forward.

T'Shaka's voice cut through the staging area, calm, steady, exact.

"Alright, team. First things first, everybody goes home."

A ripple moved through the ranks, heads lifting, shoulders squaring.

“But for that to happen,” he continued, “we move as one.”

He scanned faces, met eyes, assigned purpose with a single glance.

“We are heroes and sheroes tonight. Martinez,” he nodded to a Puerto Rican officer near the front.

She smiled, quick and fierce. “Thank you, Kid.”

Everton chuckled softly behind her. The nickname, Gonzo’s nickname, had become a badge of respect across the line.

T’Shaka continued, methodical, voice never rising.

“Switch to night vision. Every shot matter, incapacitate or neutralize. One person per squad checks vitals. We move in teams of seven.”

He pointed, mapping roles with surgical precision.

“One per squad, continuous flash and smoke deployment. One, zip ties. Lead carries the riot shield. I need two shotguns, two handguns, one rifle per stack.”

Heads nodded in unison. Pens stopped moving. They were locked in.

“Be calm. Accurate. Fast. Precise.”

He paused, just long enough for the gravity to settle over them like a second skin.

“SWAT leads entry. Shields up. We defer to experience and protect one another.”

Somewhere behind them, a generator hummed low. Helicopters hovered like held breath.

"As soon as smoke deploys," T'Shaka said, "snipers lay down cover fire. Flash follows. Then we enter."

He looked around one last time, eyes steady on every face.

"Godspeed, everybody."

A beat.

"Godspeed, Director."

Mia Strong's voice came through the earpiece, steady and proud. "Proceed."

T'Shaka smiled once, small, private, certain.

It was time.

For Omar Wells Jr.

Smoke bloomed first, thick, rolling, blinding. The night swallowed the compound whole. Flash grenades cracked like thunder, white light tearing through darkness in blinding pulses. Snipers stitched suppression fire across choke points. Shields advanced in tight formation. Boots moved in rhythm. Commands stayed low and controlled.

The Kid moved with them, never ahead, never behind, placing pieces exactly where they belonged.

Shots were counted. Hands were cuffed. Vitals were checked.

Resistance folded under precision.

And when the last door was cleared and the last shout faded into echoes, the compound fell silent, not with fear, but with finality.

T'Shaka stood still for a single breath, goggles humming softly against his temples.

Justice wasn't loud.

It was done right.

And tonight, by any means necessary, it had been.

CHAPTER TWENTY-ONE
BY ANY MEANS NECESSARY
(PART II)

For a moment, it felt like the country stopped breathing.

National networks, local affiliates, independent cameras, handheld mics crowded the perimeter as floodlights sliced through the night. Red lights blinked on every lens. Anchors whispered into earpieces. Everyone waited for the same thing.

Dr. T'Shaka Malone.

Miles away, in the Wells family home, the living room was packed—family, church elders, neighbors standing shoulder to shoulder. Christy stood near the window, hands clasped tightly, eyes lifted toward the ceiling as if she could see through the darkness.

She prayed quietly.

For the Wells family. For the community. For everyone wearing a vest tonight.

And most of all, for T'Shaka Malone.

Then the gunshots came.

Inside the compound, time fractured into commands.

MOVE. SMOKE. FLASH. MOVE.

Teams Alpha, Bravo, and Charlie flowed inward, splitting into twenty squads of seven, exactly as planned. Smoke grenades bloomed thick and choking. Flash grenades cracked like thunder, white light tearing through darkness in blinding pulses. Snipers pinned choke points with disciplined precision.

The militia fired wildly, fear replacing bravado. Some dropped weapons and fell to the ground. Others kept shooting and paid the price. The difference was immediate and unforgiving.

One man screamed into the chaos, voice breaking, “We trained for nothing!”

The words vanished under another command.

MOVE. FIRE. SMOKE. FLASH.

Over and over.

The Sons of Thunder collapsed under coordination they had never prepared for.

John Russell ran.

While his men were cut down or cuffed, he bolted for his office, heart hammering, mind racing through contingencies he had rehearsed in private. He yanked open a duffel bag stuffed with cash, wigs, passports, everything he thought would buy him distance.

He tore at a false wall and slipped through, pounding down narrow stairs toward the swamp. His boat waited below. Darkness and trees would cover his escape.

Or so he believed.

T’Shaka and Gonzo locked eyes across the chaos.

No words.

They moved.

T'Shaka had already deduced where the hidden passage would be, load-bearing inconsistencies, traffic patterns, the logic of a man who believed he was smarter than everyone else. The false wall gave way. The stairs swallowed them.

They burst into the night just as Russell stumbled toward the water.

A warning shot cracked the air, splintering the tree beside him.

"Freeze, Mr. Russell," T'Shaka called out, voice cutting clean through the swamp. "But I'd prefer you resist."

Russell dropped to his knees, gasping, playing weak. In his mind, he saw one last opening—get close, strike, run.

He lunged.

T'Shaka saw the knife instantly.

He ducked the wild swing, drove a hard kick into Russell's knee, bone snapping with a sickening crack, and fired once. The round tore through Russell's left shoulder, spinning him face-first into the mud.

It was over. Gonzo was on him in seconds, cuffs snapping shut.

They looked at each other and laughed, not from joy, from release.

Gonzo hoisted Russell over his shoulder as the defeated man screamed into the night.

Back inside the compound, order returned.

T'Shaka stepped into the command area, breath steady.

"Rodriguez," he said.

"Sir?"

"Report."

"Two agents with minor wounds. No fatalities on our side. All militia accounted for, sixty-seven deceased, one hundred twelve wounded, seventy-two in custody and secured."

T'Shaka nodded once. Another agent approached and handed him a phone.

He answered immediately.

"Yes, ma'am."

Director Strong's voice came through, controlled and proud.

"Status?"

"Mission accomplished," T'Shaka said. "No casualties. Two minor injuries."

A pause.

"Good work, Dr. Malone," she said. "Report back to the college campus for debrief and press conference."

"Yes, ma'am."

He ended the call and looked out at the night, at the quiet that followed decisive action.

Back at the Wells home, the television showed the live feed.

Christy exhaled.

Justice hadn't come easily.

But tonight, by any means necessary, it had arrived, and everyone who went in came home.

CHAPTER TWENTY-TWO
GRACE AND MERCY

Two hours later, it was officially 2000 hours, and the small town of Meridian, Mississippi was buzzing like never before.

T'Shaka had taken a quick shower, discarding his bloody, wet, mud-soaked clothes. He emerged dressed with intention: a navy-blue fitted Under Armour shirt, khaki cargo pants, and black-and-red Air Jordan 5s. His Georgetown Hoyas hat was turned backward on purpose. When he addressed the media, they would see an African American man who did not code-switch, who stood fully in himself and willingly nodded to the culture that shaped him.

Director Strong finished her briefing with Agent Gonzalez at her side. Gonzo received his flowers, then Gonzo took the microphone, he made sure the team received their credit, and most importantly, he acknowledged the Kid, correcting himself several times to properly say Dr. Malone.

T'Shaka laughed as he stepped onto the stage. He greeted his mentor, Director Strong, beautiful at fifty-five, always dressed to impress, then turned and hugged his partner, Agent Gonzalez. The room smiled at the display of emotion and brotherhood, forged through hardship and shared danger. Two men who had grown to understand one another with time.

T'Shaka stood at the podium, eyes red from the events of two hours earlier, and took the first question from Cousin Jeff of BET News.

Always thoughtful, Cousin Jeff began,

"Dr. T'Shaka Malone, first, Merry Christmas to you, your family, and all the men and women who served with you during this period."

T'Shaka smiled. It was December 22nd. He had forgotten.

"Thank you, Cousin Jeff," he replied.

Then came the defining question.

"If you could, Dr. Malone, please elaborate on your experience over the past week and a half."

T'Shaka looked into the audience. He saw everyone, then he saw the Wells family. And then he saw his mother. Her lips moved silently.

We love you. We are proud of you. Thank you.

T'Shaka had always been gifted with lip reading. He read every word.

Before he could speak, a single tear rolled down his left eye, then another from the right. Yet his voice did not waver. If anything, the tears released what might have weakened it.

"Mrs. Betty Wells, oops," he said gently, correcting himself. "Momma Wells."

The crowd laughed softly.

"Momma Wells just lost her son, Omar Wells Jr., to one of the most vile acts this country knows, lynching.

"She invited me and my partner into her home. Did you all know Momma Wells is a second-grade teacher and a choir director?" He smiled. "She reminds me so much of my own mother, who was a fourth-grade teacher and taught many of my friends and siblings."

The room leaned in.

“She made her children go to church,” T’Shaka continued, warmth returning to his voice, “but I still wonder how they stayed awake, with food as good as she cooked, it put my girl straight to sleep.”

The crowd laughed again, but something deeper settled in.

“Momma Wells taught her children well. They all sing. Omar Jr. and his dad, Big Omar as they call him, were baritones who could sing tenor or alto, depending on what was needed.”

He paused.

“As we ate, me and Gonzo heard them sing a song by the Mississippi Mass Choir. I’m no singer,” he admitted, “but these words stayed with me.”

He didn’t sing. He spoke, deep and soulful.

Your grace and mercy brought me through I’m living this moment because of You I want to thank You and praise You too Your grace and mercy brought me through

T’Shaka paused, then continued, his tone reflective rather than defensive.

“I want to be clear,” he said. “That song, Grace and Mercy, isn’t about quick forgiveness for those who’ve done wrong. It’s about discernment. About recognizing opportunities for growth during seasons of pain and reflection.”

The room was silent.

“So, Cousin Jeff,” T’Shaka continued, “this case was growth for me, and I’m sure it was growth for this entire team. I’m evolving, like every human who truly experiences life.”

He drew a steady breath.

"You see, I'm dealing with the nature of duality. I am Omar Wells Jr., because his life could have been mine. But I also hope there is never another Omar Wells Jr."

His voice strengthened.

"I choose justice as my love language. And for those who choose to hate, be their voice, and express it through harm, I will do my best to come see about your philosophy."

He nodded once.

"Thank you, Cousin Jeff. Merry Christmas to you all. Be safe."

T'Shaka stepped away from the podium.

The room rose to its feet, not in applause alone, but in understanding.

He found Christy immediately. He kissed her, then pulled her into a hug filled with relief, love, and unspoken gratitude. She returned it fully, grounding him, steadying him, reminding him he was still human beneath the weight of symbols and expectations.

The next morning, headlines spread across the US Today:

FOR OMAR WELLS JR. OUR LOVE LANGUAGE IS JUSTICE

And while the country debated, mourned, and reckoned,

Dr. T'Shaka Malone was already playing chess.

The board was set.

The case against John Russell and the Sons of Thunder had already begun mounting evidence for a corrupt city, exactly as he intended.

BONUS BOOKER T. WILLIAMS' REACTION (CHAPTER 22)

Dr. Booker T. Williams watched the speech alone.

The television volume was low, muted enough that the neighbors wouldn't hear, but loud enough that every word still landed. He sat perfectly still in the dark of his apartment, the glow from the screen painting sharp angles across his face, brilliant, composed, unreadable.

He had expected anger.

He had expected arrogance.

He had expected a child wearing a badge too big for him.

Instead, what he saw unsettled him far more.

Grace.

Not weakness, clarity.

When T'Shaka spoke about Grace and Mercy, Booker's jaw tightened. He leaned forward slightly when his brother said the words weren't about quick forgiveness, but about discernment, about growth in seasons of pain.

Booker exhaled slowly through his nose.

Careful, he thought. That's dangerous ground.

Then came the line that struck him clean through the chest.

"I am Omar Wells Jr."

Booker froze.

He felt it, not as sentiment, not as performance, but as recognition. The way a surgeon recognizes a mistake before the monitors scream. The way a predator recognizes another hunter.

He understands proximity, Booker realized. He understands inheritance.

And then the part that made his lips curve, not into rage, not into pride, but into something sharper.

“I choose justice as my love language.”

Booker let out a quiet laugh.

“Of course you do,” he murmured to the empty room.

Justice.

Clean. Public. Measured. Sanitized.

Booker stood and crossed the room, pausing by the window. Outside, the city breathed, unaware of the philosophical war being waged beneath its lights.

“You chose the long road,” he said softly. “I chose the short one.”

But even as he said it, doubt crept in, uninvited.

T’Shaka hadn’t demonized hate.

He had challenged it.

“I will do my best to come see about your philosophy.”

Booker’s smile faded.

That wasn't bravado.

That was intent.

The speech ended. Applause erupted. The camera cut away.

Booker remained standing.

For the first time since Chicago, since the acquittal, since the first sloppy kill, he felt something shift. Not fear. Not guilt.

Pressure.

His little brother wasn't reacting to chaos.

He was shaping it.

And worse, he was doing it without hatred.

Booker's fingers curled against the glass.

"You don't even know who I am," he whispered.

A beat.

"But you're already circling me."

He turned off the television.

Silence returned.

Booker walked to his desk, opened a notebook, and wrote one word at the top of a clean page:

ADAPT.

If T'Shaka's love language was justice, then Booker knew exactly what his would have to become.

Because control was everything.

And no one, not even a genius with grace, was allowed to take that from him.

Not again.

CHAPTER TWENTY-THREE (Bonus)— LOVE LANGUAGE

Christy woke up to the sound of CNN.

Not music. Not laughter. Debate.

A panel filled the screen, journalists, politicians, academics, familiar faces. The chyron read:

LOVE LANGUAGE: JUSTICE VS. HATE

Christy squinted, still half-asleep, and pulled the hotel sheet closer around her shoulders.

Cousin Jeff was speaking.

He leaned forward in his chair, smiling, not smug, but proud.

"Last night," Cousin Jeff said, "Dr. T'Shaka Malone did something rare. He gave us a master class in philosophy. The way Black preaching does it, he introduced the argument, built the tension, and closed with clarity."

One of the panelists nodded. Another tried to interrupt.

Cousin Jeff waved them off gently.

"I love this man," he continued. "This kid. This FBI agent. This activist. This Black man. He didn't shout. He didn't posture. He defined harm and then told us what love looks like when it refuses to tolerate it."

A senator chimed in about optics.

A pundit tried to reduce it to sound bites.

A professor talked about moral duality.

Christy yawned.

She stretched.

And then she noticed something.

Her hand.

Her left hand.

There was a ring on her finger.

Her eyes widened.

She sat straight up.

Silence filled the room, just for a second.

Then,

“AAAAAAAAAAHHHHHHHH!”

She screamed.

She screamed again.

And then she screamed the only name that mattered.

“T’SHAKA MALONE!”

Footsteps.

Quick. Calm. Familiar.

T’Shaka walked into the presidential suite wearing Georgetown Hoyas pajama pants and his Malcolm X T-shirt. His hair was in a tight fade, with a cool ass part on the side. His breath smelled like toothpaste. He looked entirely too peaceful for someone who had just detonated her entire world.

He leaned against the doorway.

“You may wanna brush your teeth before we scream again,” he said, smiling.

“BOY,” Christy shouted, already running past him into the bathroom.

She brushed furiously, slipping into one of T’Shaka’s old TSU alumni shirts, long enough to be a nightgown on her, soft and worn in the best way.

She walked back out, heart pounding.

She held up her hand.

“What,” she said slowly, “are you asking me, T’Shaka Malone?”

He didn’t joke.

He didn’t deflect.

He walked toward her.

“I already spoke to your father,” he said. “And your brother. Before we left Nashville, I was going to ask after that crazy ass movie but, we were interrupted. This case dropped on me fast, but I needed them to know.”

Christy’s breath caught.

“They gave me their blessing.”

He reached into his pocket, not for another ring, but for certainty, and then he dropped to one knee.

Christy covered her mouth tears falling, heart beating fast.

In his deep voice, “Christy Jones,” T’Shaka said softly, steadily, “you’ve been my best friend since first grade. You’ve protected me when the world tried to label me. You’ve grounded me when my mind tried to run away from my heart.”

He looked up at her, fully present.

“I choose you because I love you with all my heart and soul,” he said. “And I want you to know that I got your back for the rest of our natural lives.”

A beat.

“So, Christy Jones, will you marry me?”

The world outside kept arguing.

Inside the suite, love finally had the floor.

CHAPTER TWENTY-THREE CONTINUED

The next three days moved slowly, as if time itself understood it needed to be gentle.

Christmas was spent with the Wells family.

No cameras. No microphones. Just people who had been wounded and were learning how to breathe again. There was laughter, soft and cautious, and there were moments when silence said more than words ever could. T'Shaka stayed present, not as an agent, not as a symbol, but as a young man sitting at a table where grief and grace shared the same space.

Then came the funeral.

Omar Wells Jr.'s homegoing service filled the church to capacity. People stood along the walls. Others listened from outside, speakers carrying hymns into the cold Mississippi air. Law enforcement from across the state attended, uniforms mixed with suits, heads bowed without rank.

Even Director Mia Strong sat quietly in the pews.

The service was beautiful. Short. Honest.

No spectacle. No politics.

Just love, loss, and remembrance.

When T'Shaka spoke with the family afterward, he did not come with prepared remarks. He came with resolve.

He told them he was making a one-million-dollar donation, not in Omar's name for charity, but for legacy.

The plans were already drawn.

The school would be called:

Omar Wells Jr. School of Exceptional Children

A place unlike anything the Black community had ever seen.

Pre-K through sixth grade. Technologically advanced classrooms. A state-of-the-art music room. A CSI and forensic science lab designed to spark curiosity early.

T'Shaka had already drafted the blueprints himself.

When he showed them, the Wells family wept openly. So did members of the community. The grief did not disappear, but it transformed. It found direction.

The town responded with gratitude so fierce it surprised everyone. Big Omar called to T'Shaka: Son… Thank you for everything, please don't be a stranger maybe we will teach you how to play the piano.

T'Shaka laughed. "Mr. Wells, I taught myself last night at the hotel, who knows maybe I will accompany the Wells.

Mr. Wells laughed and could be heard saying something about smart Alec genius.

There was talk of naming a street after Dr. T'Shaka Malone and Agent Gonzalez.

Gonzo tried to brush it off. Tried to be tough.

Failed miserably.

He cried like a baby, hard, unapologetic tears, and didn't stop until they crossed the state line out of Mississippi.

“I hate y’all,” he muttered, wiping his face. “I really do.”

T’Shaka just smiled.

Gonzo returned to Virginia to spend time with his family, finally letting himself rest.

T’Shaka and Christy went back to Nashville, savoring the quiet days before Christy returned to Spelman for her second semester. Her GPA stood at a perfect 4.0, and she carried it with the same confidence she carried everything else.

Before work resumed and calendars filled again, T’Shaka went home.

His mother’s house.

He sat on the floor playing with his two nieces, daughters of his oldest sister. He laughed with his cousins. Talked with his grandfather. Beat his father in basketball. Ate too much food. Let himself be just family.

Christy fit in as if she had always belonged, because she had.

She watched him in those moments: son, uncle, cousin, fiancé. Not the prodigy. Not the agent. Just T’Shaka.

And for the first time in weeks, the weight lifted.

Not because the world was fixed.

But because love had done what it always did best.

It reminded them what, and who, was worth fighting for.

FINAL CHAPTER TWENTY-FOUR THE PIVOT

POV: Dr. Booker T. Atticus Williams

Booker T. Atticus Williams had learned long ago that control was not rigidity.

Control was knowing when to pivot.

He stood in the quiet of his apartment, the city humming beneath him, reading—not watching, but studying—everything his little brother had done since Meridian. The press conferences. The speeches that turned philosophy into quiet thunder. The chess moves disguised as compassion. The way T'Shaka bent systems without ever laying a hand on them.

Booker smiled. His little brother was not merely brilliant.

He was dangerous.

And Booker respected danger.

It was time to pivot.

T'Shaka had proven to be more than a challenge. His intellect knew no ceiling, his morality no hesitation. Booker understood now—direct opposition would fail. This wasn't a man to be outpaced or outgunned. He would have to be learned. Studied. Mirrored. Then surpassed.

So Booker stepped back.

He cleaned.

Loose ends first.

The secretary of the Mississippi NAACP never saw it coming.

Booker didn't rush it. He never did when the message mattered. He watched, waited, confirmed patterns. When it was over, there was no chaos—only consequence.

Even Black-led organizations, Booker believed, were not immune from accountability.

Especially when they allowed institutions to do what should have been done decades ago.

The death would be framed as tragic. Confusing. Unresolved.

Booker washed his hands of Mississippi.

Then he began to build.

His first call was to his best friend—the one who had assisted him in Texas. The one who had quietly hijacked every CCTV camera in a three-mile radius while a judge bled out behind closed doors.

A ghost in the machine.

"I'm restructuring," Booker said calmly. "I need you."

There was no hesitation on the other end.

"I'm in."

Booker already had four more names in mind.

Doctors. Engineers. Analysts. Believers.

A team.

But before any of that could take shape, another hand moved across the board.

UTAH

The room was private.

The men inside were not accustomed to secrecy—but tonight required it.

Mordecai Russell sat at the head of the table, knuckles white, jaw clenched. John Russell had been his brother's son. Blood.

Good blood.

And now he was gone.

"They prosecuted," Mordecai said slowly, "and they killed good white men."

The others nodded.

Politicians. Donors. Power brokers.

Men who smiled on camera and plotted in shadow.

"And they did it," Mordecai continued, "because they let one man rise too far. Too fast."

A name was spoken.

Dr. T'Shaka Malone.

No one interrupted.

"No man," Mordecai said, "should hold that much power. Not at eighteen. Not ever."

Silence followed.

Then agreement.

Quiet. Calculated. Deadly.

Decisions were made that night—ones that would not reach the public, not yet. Strings would be pulled. Narratives rewritten. Institutions weaponized against themselves.

Law enforcement would fracture.

Trust would erode.

If necessary, the country itself would be pushed toward something darker.

Not because of justice.

But because of fear.

Booker T. Williams looked out over the city as the sun rose, gold bleeding across steel and glass.

His brother stood on one side of history, armed with law, love, and an unshakable belief in justice.

Booker stood on the other—armed with patience, control, and inevitability.

And now, unseen forces were moving between them.

He smiled softly.

“Let the game begin,” he whispered.

END OF BOOK ONE

T’Shaka will return for **Book II: Two Sides of The Same Coin – By Any Means Necessary**

Author's Notes

by Dr. TJ Debnam

Two Sides of the Same Coin: What Is Harm?

Book I of the Dr. T'Shaka Malone Series

This book was born from a question that would not let me go.

What is harm—and who gets to define it?

We live in a world where violence is often loud, but harm is frequently quiet. It hides behind policies, traditions, legal language, and moral certainty. It wears uniforms. It carries credentials. And sometimes, it insists it is necessary.

Two Sides of the Same Coin is not just a thriller—it is a moral investigation. Through Dr. T'Shaka Malone, I wanted to explore what happens when brilliance meets systems that were never designed to protect it, and when justice confronts the uncomfortable truth that the law and morality are not always aligned.

T'Shaka is young, gifted, and burdened—not because genius is rare, but because society often treats extraordinary Black intellect as either a threat or a tool. His story is not about perfection. It is about **discernment**. About learning how to stand inside duality without losing oneself. About choosing justice not as vengeance, but as responsibility.

The antagonist in this story is not simply a killer. He is an ideology—one that believes harm can be justified if it serves order, purity, or control. That belief is not fictional. It exists in hospitals, courtrooms, boardrooms, and history books. This novel asks the reader to wrestle with that reality, not from a distance, but from within.

Book I asks the question.

Book II will confront the cost of the answer.

I wrote this story for those who understand that justice is rarely comfortable, that love can be disruptive, and that moral clarity often arrives only after we sit with uncomfortable truths.

Thank you for reading.

Thank you for questioning.

And thank you for walking with Dr. T'Shaka Malone into the space where certainty ends—and responsibility begins.

— **Dr. TJ Debnam**

Dedication

This book is dedicated to my mother, Patricia Malone, who from an early age encouraged imagination, reading, and the freedom to pursue whatever path called to me, always with love, patience, and belief.

To my lovely sisters, whose presence, strength, and support have always surrounded me.

To my son, Tyriq Debnam, my greatest source of inspiration and my constant reminder to be better than I was yesterday.

And to my family, near, far, and beyond sight, who continue to pour into me and walk alongside me.

It is a rare and beautiful blessing to have such a great number of clouds of witnesses.